The Singing Sleuth
Runs a B&B

The Singing Sleuth Runs a B&B

D.B. Barton

Usher Press

New York   Jacksonville

The Singing Sleuth Runs a B&B

by D.B. Barton

Copyright 2022
Cover by Barbara Lambros

The Singing Sleuth Print Series:

The Singing Sleuth (2005, 2012)
The Singing Sleuth Returns (2007, 2014)
The Singing Sleuth Goes Home (2009, 2017)
The Singing Sleuth Crosses the Pond (2011, 2021)
The Singing Sleuth Does Vegas (2013)
The Singing Sleuth Takes a Bow (2016)
The Singing Sleuth Meets His Matches (2020)
The Singing Sleuth Runs a B&B (2022)
The Singing Sleuth Finds a Leaf (2023)

The complete series can be ordered directly from
www.singingsleuth.com.

Printed in the United States of America

To the women in my church's crochet group
who have:

Sampled my baked goods,
Helped me invent my characters,
and
Encouraged me to be who God created me to be.

Contents

▼

Land's End B&B: First Floor

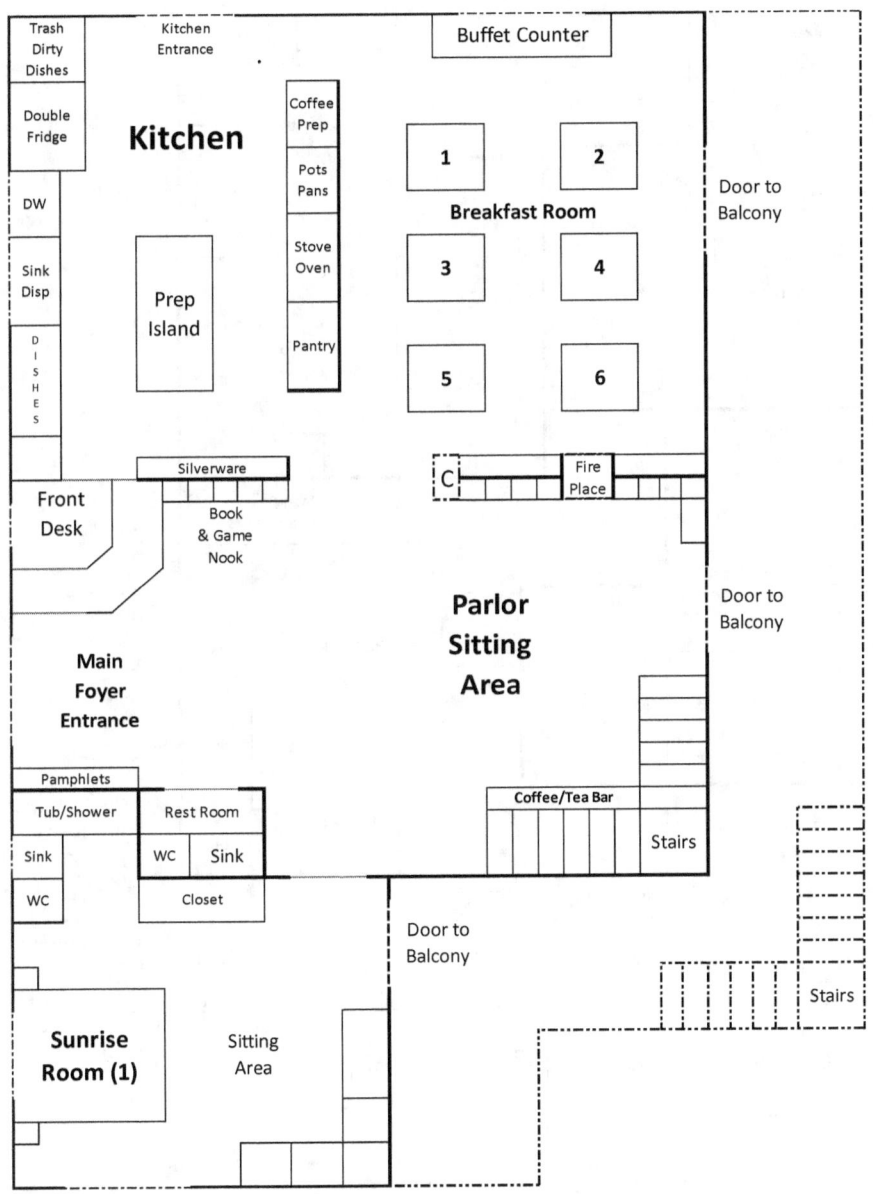

Land's End B&B: Second Floor

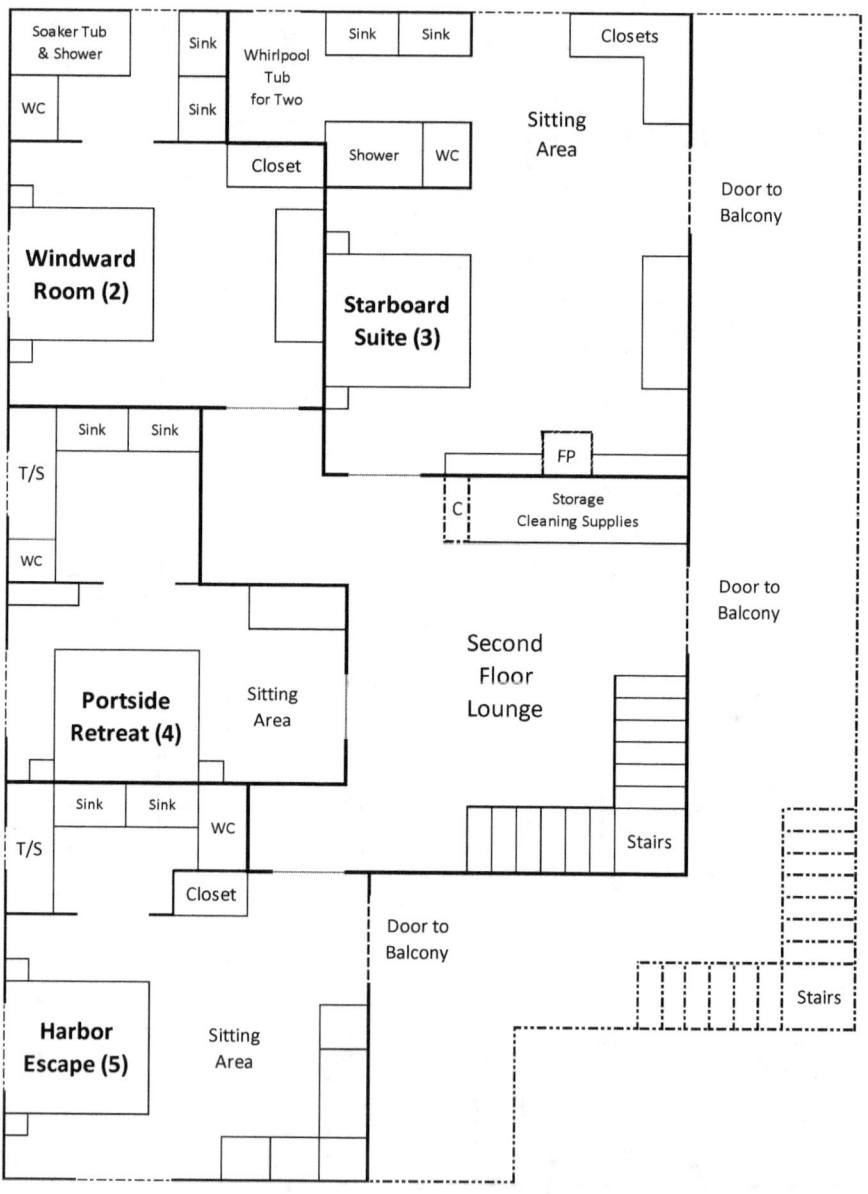

Land's End B&B: Third Floor

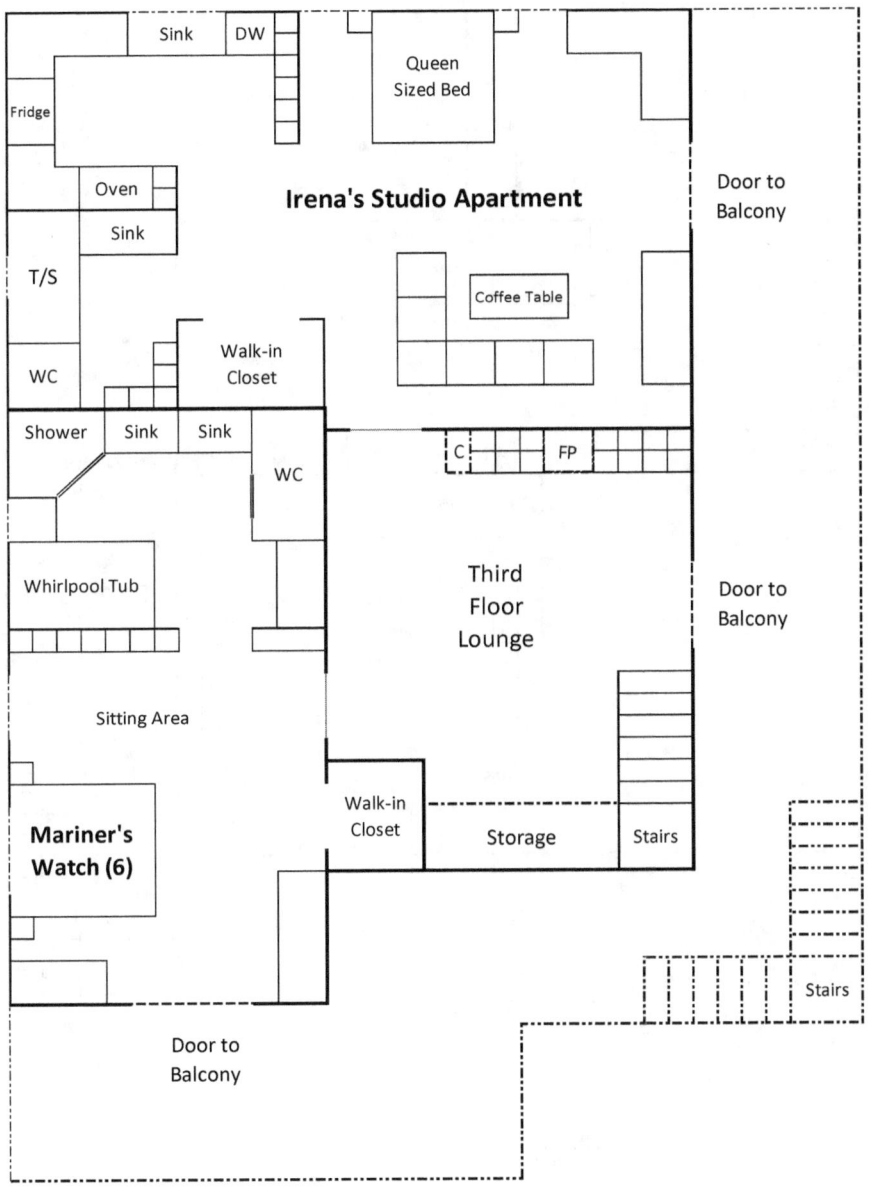

Land's End B&B: Lower Level

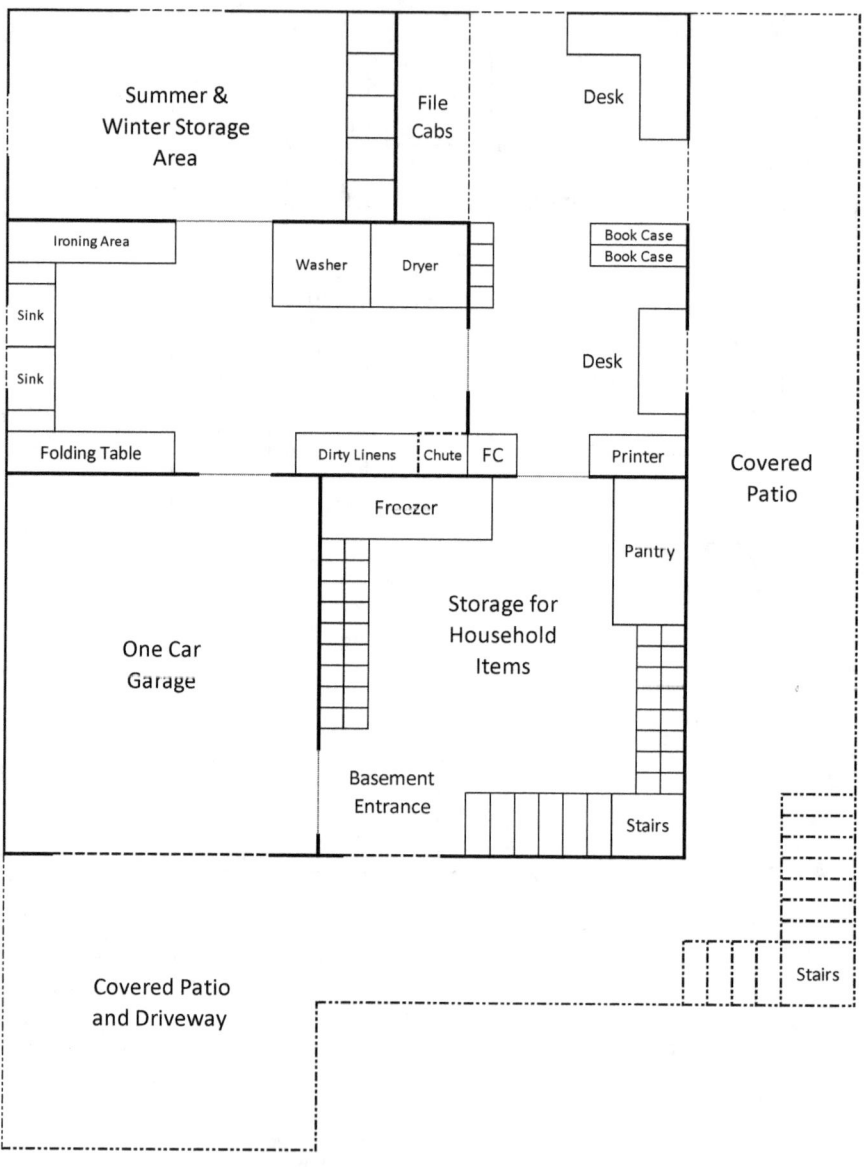

Land's End B&B
Room Descriptions, Rates, and Amenities

Sunrise Room (#1)

The Sunrise Room was part of the original 1885 inn and is exquisitely appointed. It has a king-sized bed with a private bathroom (tub/shower and single sink). The room is located on our first floor in the southwest corner of the inn. It is close to the front desk, library, parlor, and breakfast room. The Sunrise Room has a spectacular view of Boothbay Harbor and its surroundings. Guests have private access to the inn's full-length, covered balcony.
The summer rate for the Sunrise Room is $295.00 per night.

Windward Room (#2)

The Windward Room has a large picture window that overlooks our lovely summer garden. It has interior access to the inn's full-length balcony, which offers breathtaking views of the inner harbor. The room is on the second floor in the northwest corner of the inn. It is close to the landing's airy lounge and indoor staircase. The Windward Room contains a king-sized bed and a modern bathroom with a soaker tub/shower and double sinks.
The summer rate for the Windward Room is $265.00 per night.

Starboard Suite (#3)

The Starboard Suite is one of our most romantic and largest accommodations. The suite is located on the second floor in the northeast corner of the inn. It contains a canopied king-sized bed, a cozy sitting area, and an electric fireplace that can warm you on cool New England nights. The luxurious bathroom contains a whirlpool tub for two, a large, separate shower with two heads, and

double sinks. Guests can access the inn's full-length, covered balcony through their own private door.
The summer rate for the Starboard Suite is $325.00 per night.

Portside Retreat (#4)

The Portside Retreat has a large picture window that overlooks our charming garden entrance. The room was part of the original inn that was built in 1885. It's located on the second floor in the northwest portion of the inn and has access to the landing's airy lounge, inside staircase, and full-length, covered balcony. The Portside Retreat has a cozy sitting area and a sleek bathroom with a tub/shower and double sinks.
The summer rate for the Portside Retreat is $265.00 per night.

Harbor Escape (#5)

Harbor Escape has a southwest exposure on the second floor of the inn. It is a little larger than the Sunrise Room, which sits beneath it. Guests can enjoy the same spectacular views of our scenic inner harbor from sunrise to sunset. The room has direct access to the inn's full-length balcony. Harbor Escape is a romantic hideaway with a canopied king-sized bed and a bathroom that includes a tub/shower and double sinks. It, too, was part of the original inn built in 1885.
The summer rate for the Harbor Escape is $295.00 per night.

Mariner's Watch (#6)

Marine's Watch has just been renovated and is our largest and most private accommodation. It is located on the third floor and has 270° panoramic views of the summer garden and our sparkling blue harbor. It contains a king-sized bed, a walk-in closet, and a cozy sitting room. The luxurious bathroom has a whirlpool tub for two, a separate shower, and double sinks. Mariner's Watch has private access to the balcony, which looks out upon Boothbay Harbor and its beautiful surroundings.

The summer rate for the Starboard Suite is $325.00 per night.

Land's End Amenities

Our three-deck balcony runs the complete length of the Land's End Inn and gives our guests breathtaking views of Boothbay Harbor. Four of our six rooms have direct access to the balcony, and all guests are encouraged to have breakfast, afternoon tea, cocktails, and snacks on our decks.

Each deck contains multiple seating areas with patio tables and padded chairs. The outside staircase has a sleek and safe cable railing from which guests can view their surroundings while also giving them privacy to come and go from their rooms as they please.

Our complimentary hot breakfast is served between 8:30 AM and 10:00 AM. Upon request, early risers or those catching flights can obtain coffee, tea, juice, cold cereal, and homemade baked goods in the breakfast room from 7:00 AM to 8:30 AM. Hot breakfast is served in the breakfast room and al fresco on the first-floor balcony.

We look forward to pampering you with the finest ingredients and local Maine produce in both our savory and sweet dishes. For the convenience of our guests, the breakfast menu for the following morning can be viewed the previous evening on a blackboard near the reception desk.

Includes:
Free Parking
Free Wi-Fi
Comfortable Parlors on every floor
Afternoon Snacks in the first-floor parlor
Air Conditioning/Heat
Ceiling Fans

Flat Screen Satellite TVs
Mini Fridges with Ice and Barware
Single Pod Coffee and Tea Makers
Modern, Spacious Bathrooms
Gilchrist and Soames Toiletries
Hair Dryers
Egyptian Cotton Bath Towels
Comfy Robes on request
Luxury Linens
Cozy Comforters
Seating on the Waterfront Lawn

PROLOGUE

▼

Saturday Evening
2nd of July
8:46 PM EDT

"We've finished the first leg of our journey," Paige sighed. "Are you hungry? We have time to grab something to eat. Our flight to Portland, Maine is not going to depart until ten, and Gate 49 is just down the terminal."

Alec smiled, "You know I'm always hungry, Lass. Let's see what delicacies we can get in JFK Airport."

Toting hand luggage, Alec and Paige walked past a few gates and commented about the shops and food stations." Alec checked his watch. "It's 9:00 PM now. I don't want to have anything too heavy, maybe just a burger."

Paige, Alec's wife of eighteen months, agreed as she stopped by a posted menu in front of Urban Crave. "At this time of night, I don't want to overeat either. Their club sandwich sounds good to me, and this restaurant specializes in Bloody Marys."

Alec winked. "Who are you? And what have you done with my wife? I'm usually the one who likes to pair my food with alcoholic beverages."

Paige sighed for a second time since arriving in New York City. With a frown, she admitted, "I'm a bit worried about Aunt Irena. She's in her mid-seventies and pretty frail. A broken ankle can change how a person ages. In the past, Irena has always been so lively. Out of all my aunts and uncles, she's my favorite."

Alec steered Paige into the eatery. After they ordered, Alec prompted, "Let me see your father's email again."

Paige reached into her handbag's side pocket and pulled out a folded piece of paper. Alec took it from her hand and read quietly:

Subj: Aunt Irena
Date: 26th of June, 04:03:48 PM PST
From: RAnderson@aol.com
To: PaigeDunBarton@aol.com

Sweetheart,

I know you and Alec are planning to fly out to me next Sunday, but I think it may be wise for you to change those plans. This afternoon, I heard from your Aunt Irena, She's in the hospital with a fractured ankle and a sprained wrist. She fell off her kitchen stepladder earlier today while reaching for something on an upper shelf.

Although Irena has a housekeeper to do the heavy work at her bed and breakfast, she's afraid that she won't be able to run the inn effectively. She's also worried about pleasing one of her more difficult guests who is staying for a month.

Aunt Irena is getting on in years and needs some help making breakfast and seeing to the comfort of her guests. I thought of you two right away. I know Alec loves to cook and, Paige, you're marvelous with people. Maine is beautiful this time of the year. As you may remember, the inn contains six guest rooms with ensuite bathrooms. Irena just finished renovating the large third-floor suite and I'm sure it would suit you and Alec perfectly. The room has a birds-eye view of Boothbay Harbor.

Let me know whether you can rescue Aunt Irena. If you're able, call me tonight. I don't think you'll have much trouble exchanging your airline tickets to California for those to Maine. I hope Irena will be fully recuperated from her injuries this August to join us on our family cruise. I'm going to call your aunt tomorrow to see how she's faring.

Lots of Love,
Dad

Hoping to be encouraging, Alec added. "That was nearly a week ago. Since then, we have changed our flights, spoken to your dad twice, and heard directly from Aunt Irena. She's back at home and her housekeeper and neighbors have pitched in to help her. She's in good hands, and when we get there, you'll have nothing to worry about."

Alec kept his concerns to himself. Although Alec's family owned and operated the DunBarton Inn in Inverness, Scotland, Alec was less than confident that he could run a bed and breakfast. He liked to cook and bake but was known to add and remove important ingredients from recipes on a whim. His meals and baked goods were either exceptionally good or terribly bad.

Smiling since they arrived in the airport, Paige concurred. "Irena seems to be on the mend. I just wish we could go directly there instead of waiting till tomorrow."

The food arrived as Alec was about to reply. After tasting his draft beer, Alec watched Paige take a sip of her Bloody Mary and said, "Let's call your aunt before our next flight leaves at ten. If she needs us right away, we'll rent a car at Portland International Jetport and go tonight."

The DunBartons enjoyed their meal. Realizing that she was hungrier than she thought, Paige took a few of Alec's fries off his plate with a sly glance.

Noting that she looked fetching, Alec winked. "If we're not needed until tomorrow morning, we can enjoy our last night together at the motel we booked in Portland. Our second flight is scheduled to land in Portland at eleven thirty. Even though Boothbay Harbor is just an hour away from the airport, I'd rather not drive when it's dark and we're tired."

Unsure whether her husband was in the mood for romance or just being sensible, Paige yawned. "I am weary. I think I've been running on adrenaline the last few days."

The DunBarton's second flight was called on time. As the pair settled in the seats of their small plane, Paige happily shared the conversation she just had with Irena. Paige reported that her aunt's guests were in for the night. For the last few days, her housekeeper, Karine, had been a great help, preparing breakfasts as well as fulfilling her other household duties.

Thrilled, Alec asked, "Does that mean we don't have to cook?"

Paige shook her head, "No, it just means we don't have to cook tomorrow. Irena plans to be right by your side when you have to make her various egg dishes, frittatas, quiches, and cakes. Karine will continue to do the heavy work, but her husband, a lobsterman, has missed her while she's been taking care of my aunt at night."

"I can understand that!" Alec pronounced. "Does Irena have any other helpers?"

Trying to remember everything that was said, Paige recalled, "Aunt Irena's neighbor is also her bookkeeper. She's a single mom, and her son, Patrick, is very interested in becoming an actor. He plans to go to college this autumn and is currently working at the inn's reception desk."

Suddenly laughing, Paige added, "Don't be surprised if you hear him take phone reservations using a variety of accents. I'm told his English, Scottish, and Irish accents sound authentic."

Alec, a born and bred Scotsman, snorted, "We'll see! Is there anything else I should know?"

Resting her head against Alec's shoulder, Paige mumbled, "Not really. Irena is sending Patrick to pick us up tomorrow. He should get to our motel by eleven…ish."

CHAPTER ONE

▼

"Summer Breeze"
Words & Music by Jim Seals and Dash Crofts
Genre: Soft Rock, Released: August 1972

Sunday Morning—3rd of July

Alec and Paige DunBarton had their suitcases lined up in front of the motel when a young man, driving a Hyundai Elantra, pulled up to the entrance. When he stepped out of the car, the fellow theatrically removed his chauffer's cap with a bow and said with a cultured English accent, "You're the DunBartons. I'm Patrick Bishop, here to whisk you away to the Land's End Bed and Breakfast in Boothbay Harbor."

Paige started to giggle as the lad gallantly reached for Paige's hand and kissed it. Alec couldn't help smiling as Patrick saluted him and then opened the car's rear door for Paige to get in. Alec watched him as he stowed their luggage into the trunk and tried to stuff his wavy black hair back under his chauffer's cap.

Patrick was tall and lean. Only a few pimples on his forehead detracted from the lad's good looks. Alec, wanting to see Maine's beauty and coastline from the passenger's front seat, asked his wife, "Do you mind, Lass?"

Happy to look around from the backseat, Paige answered, "Not at all." Dreamily, she added, "It's wonderful to be in Maine again."

Alec was quiet as Patrick ably maneuvered the car onto I-295 North. As they left Portland behind, Alec caught sight of tranquil blue harbors nestled between land masses that jutted into the Atlantic.

It wasn't long before Patrick caught them up on all the latest news. Over the next thirty minutes, he let them know that Irena was doing fine and had insisted on manning the front desk while he was picking them up.

The young man had a way of making the most mundane things sound extremely engrossing by modifying the pitch of his voice and the speed in which he spoke. Alec was not surprised when Patrick proudly announced, "I'm going to be performing in *The Importance of Being Ernest* at the end of this month with my theater group. I hope you can help me run my lines. I have a large part as Algernon Moncrieff."

Paige cried out in delight, "That's wonderful! I love that play and the satirical way that Oscar Wilde brought attention to the outlandish social obligations that the upper crust in Victorian England had to endure. It will be great to see you on stage, and we'll help you in any way we can."

Alec agreed and asked about the guests who were currently staying at Land's End.

With enthusiasm, Patrick rattled off, "There's Hillary Fairchild. She's English and very sexy for a middled-aged woman. I think she's an interior decorator. She usually visits in the fall, but this year, she came earlier.

"The Pierces always come in July and usually stay ten days. They've been coming for years. They like to visit sights around Boothbay Harbor. Dr. Pierce is a 'kindly old gent.'"

Patrick changed is accent at the latter end of his sentence and then continued in his normal voice, "His wife, Leanne, is a bit scatter-brained. She fidgets a lot and laughs at the wrong times. My mom said she's an empty nester, whatever that is.

"The other guest rooms are filled with two-nighters. They come and go as they please and it's nearly impossible to remember much about them. That just leaves *him*!"

Alec gazed at Patrick's profile as he uttered the last word. Although, he could only see half his face, Alec was able to make out a distinct sneer.

It was Paige who queried, "Him? Are you talking about that difficult guest Aunt Irena has been worried about?"

Lowering his voice as if telling a secret, Patrick answered, "*Him,* is his Honor, Judge Richard Cassidy. He lives in Boothbay Harbor but is staying at Land's End until all the black mold from his posh house on Alley Road has been removed.

Alec glanced back at Paige. Noting her pinched expression, Alec tried to lighten the mood and said, "He can't be that bad, can he?"

Patrick simply responded, "Worse."

The scenery changed as the car merged onto U.S. Route 1 North near Brunswick. As the road twisted and turned, Patrick explained that in just a thirty-mile radius in the mid coast of Maine, there were five peninsulas with over three thousand miles of coastline. Alec had a hard time imagining it until Patrick passed him a map showing the many inlets and coves.

Paige seconded Patrick's comment that Boothbay Harbor was voted one of the prettiest villages in the state. In response to Alec's question about what he and Paige could do on their free time, Patrick listed off, "There are lots of lighthouses, antique shops, a botanical garden, a railway museum, and a bunch of boat excursions. And," he added, "If you don't mind driving three hours each way, you must visit Acadia National Park in Bar Harbor."

Eagerly, Paige touched Alec's shoulder from the backseat and exclaimed, "I'd like to visit Bar Harbor. Even though Aunt Irena took me to some of those sights, it would be really nice to see them with you."

Alec caught her excitement when the car crossed over the Sheepscot River in Wiscasset and turned onto Route 27 South.

Along the road the DunBartons saw pottery barns, farm stands, antique stores, and signs for yard sales. Closer to the town of Boothbay Harbor, Alec called out, "Is Hannaford's a grocery store and do they sell Glenlivet?"

Patrick looked at Alec in a perplexed manner while Paige explained, "You'll learn that my husband loves to eat and drink. His favorite beverage is single-malt Scotch whisky. Alec also sings whenever the spirit moves him. I don't think anyone will get murdered while we're here, but song lyrics help him figure out who did what to whom."

The young man laughed awkwardly and replied, "In that case, you'll be happy to know that Boothbay Harbor is a peaceful place and that grocery stores in Maine sell liquor." Patrick then turned up several hills in succession and descended another toward the seaport town. Slowing down, he added, "Land's End Inn is right up this street."

When Patrick turned into the inn's driveway and stopped the car, Paige jumped out of the backseat with great exuberance and hurried up the steps to the B&B's foyer. Aunt Irena was in a wheelchair parked at the entrance. Though Alec was behind his wife, he could see Irena beaming. Her eyes sparkled as they alighted on her niece and with outstretched arms, she embraced Paige.

When they finally separated, Alec took in Irena's appearance. She was a petite woman and appeared very frail in her wheelchair. Her white hair was cut short, in a wispy style that delicately framed her oval face.

"So, this is your husband," Irena cooed. "Paige, I approve." Winking at Alec, she said to him, "Yes, I can see you're perfect for my favorite niece."

Although Irena appeared to be fragile, her manner was anything but. Her voice was soft, but it exuded strength and clarity. Her blue eyes were sharp and seemed to take in everything around her. Beneath her demure façade, Aunt Irena was wise and shrewd.

Using both her injured wrist in a cast and her good arm, Irena wheeled her chair away from the inn's foyer to allow Patrick to enter with the DunBarton's largest suitcase. Irena instructed, "Take that up to Mariner's Watch, dear. Once that's done, I'd like you to give Paige and Alec a tour of the inn and grounds."

Patrick saluted with a wide smile and said in a German accent, *"Ja vol mein fraulein."*

Irena smiled indulgently. "He's going to be a wonderful actor. And he's so good with our guests."

Alec excused himself to get the rest of their luggage from the car and followed Patrick up the stairs to the third floor of the Land's End Inn. On the second landing, Alec caught up with Patrick and murmured, "This place is larger than I had expected."

"Wait till you see your suite," Patrick replied. "Miss Irena just had it renovated and it has the most amazing views of the inner harbor and town."

On the third landing, Alec's eyes took in the cozy sitting room and gas fireplace. When he peeked through the glass panes of the French doors leading to the third-floor balcony, he swore, "Bloody Hell! I can see for miles."

Patrick agreed. The view was remarkable and showed Alec the door to Irena's studio apartment, explaining, "We don't have an elevator at the inn. Miss Irena is currently staying in the Sunrise Room. It's on the first floor."

While opening the door to the DunBarton's suite. Patrick bowed and said, "Voila!"

The room was beautifully appointed with large windows, floor-length curtains, and a king-sized bed with a fluffy duvet and colorful soft cushions. The furniture and dressers had a beachy distressed look but were, nevertheless, pleasing to the eye and restful to the soul. The suite also contained a slender refrigerator, a table and two chairs, a single-serving coffee machine, and bar paraphernalia.

After setting down the luggage, Alec peeked into the walk-in closet and spa-like bathroom and sighed, "Paige will love it. When she visited her aunt in the past, this floor was unfinished. As a child, she thought the attic was haunted by her great grandpa, Yuri."

Patrick laughed. "When I had to get things out of storage, I used to hear the sound of rustling chains. Before we go back downstairs, you must see your private balcony. It's right out here."

He drew open the drapes to reveal another set of French doors that faced an outdoor seating area. Alec stepped onto the deck, followed by Patrick. The southwestern view of the inner harbor was astounding, and the gentle summer breezes brought the Seals and Crofts tune to Alec's mind. Wistfully, he sang out,

Summer breeze makes me feel fine
Blowin' through the jasmine in my mind
Summer breeze makes me feel fine
Blowin' through the jasmine in my mind

Sweet days of summer, the jasmine's in bloom
July is dressed up and playing her tune
And I come home from a hard day's work
And you're waitin' there
Not a care in the world

See the smile awaitin' in the kitchen
Through cookin' and the plates for two
Feel the arms that reach out to hold me
In the evening when the day is through

Summer breeze makes me feel fine
Blowing through the jasmine in my mind
Summer breeze makes me feel fine
Blowing through the jasmine in my mind

Since Patrick had been forewarned, he did not seem too surprised and commented, "You're a great singer. Have you ever thought of performing on stage?"

Alec grinned in response. Now eager to see how Paige was faring, the two men took the outdoor staircase down to the first-floor parlor. Paige was seated on the sectional next to her aunt and heard Irena complain, "I was feeling my seventy-five years before the accident. I don't know how much longer I'll be able to run the inn. Joan, Patrick's mom, wants to buy it, but she's been unable to get a mortgage from the bank. I would hate to see it go to a stranger."

Patting Paige's shoulder, she added, "Don't let my ramblings spoil your mood."

Gazing up at the newcomers, Irena directed Patrick, "Show Paige and Alec the kitchen first and that list we made together. And, whatever, you do," she impishly smiled, "Make sure they don't flee when they see how much there is to do to operate a successful bed and breakfast."

While Irena was maneuvering her wheelchair back to the front desk, she added, "When you finish your tour and get a chance to freshen up, come back here. You must be getting hungry, and we have so much to catch up on."

In the breakfast room, Paige noted the blackboard menu for the following day and remarked to Alec, "You're going to be busy tomorrow. Do you think you'll be able to make a spinach frittata and strawberry waffles?"

Full of confidence, "Alec replied, "It shouldn't be a problem." Less sure of himself, he asked, "What is cinnamon babka? Do I have to make that too?"

Patrick ushered them into the kitchen saying, "I think we have enough frozen bread and cake to last a few more days. By that time, you should be an old hand."

Alec felt better as he gazed at the fully equipped kitchen. It had a large stainless-steel island in the center of the room, a commercial refrigerator, a double oven, and deep farmhouse sink. Paige was drawn to the coffee prep area and exclaimed, "It's well stocked, and there are pots and pans of every description in the cabinets. I'm sure you'll feel at home here very soon."

Patrick went on to show them the outdoor kitchen exit and the small pass through to the front desk. He also explained that it was safer to enter the kitchen from one door and exit it through another.

To digest all the information, Patrick, Alec, and Paige sat down at a table in the breakfast room to review Irena's list of daily and weekly duties. Almost afraid to look, Alec read:

Weekly Schedule

Week of : _____

		Mon	Tues	Wed	Thu	Fri	Sat	Sun
Morning: (7:00 AM to 11:00 AM)								
Alec	Bring in newspapers							
Alec	Turn off outside lights							
Paige	Tidy up first floor parlor							
Paige	Remove trash from first floor balcony							
Alec	Turn on warming drawer for breads, cooked bacon, sausage, etc.							
Alec	Make coffee, and put out hot beverages and pitchers of juice for the buffet counter							
Alec	Make breakfast entrees							
Paige	Fill the guest baskets with creams, pots of jams, and pats of butter							
Paige	Serve breakfast							
Paige	Clear tables							
Paige	Bring in dirty dishes							
Paige	Empty trash cans							
Paige	Empty juice pitchers							
Paige	Clean off buffet counter							
Alec	Put away unused food							
Alec	Load dishwasher							
Alec	Bake cakes for afternoon tea							

		Mon	Tues	Wed	Thu	Fri	Sat	Sun
Early Afternoon: 11:00 PM to 3:00 PM								
Patrick	Answer questions and concerns at check out							
Patrick	Open computer program							
Patrick	Check out guests on property management software							
Patrick	Check credit card batch report and match							
Patrick	Send welcome email to guests arriving in a week							
Alec	Finish baking (breads, muffins, or cakes)							
Alec	Restock pantry and refrigerator items							
Alec	Update grocery list							
Alec	Clean kitchen							
Alec	Run dishwasher							
Alec	Takeout kitchen trash							
Paige	Help wherever needed							
Karine	Flip or Fluff rooms							
Karine	Vacuum floors and steps							
Karine	Do laundry (sheets, towels, bathrobes, etc.)							
Karine	Iron and fold laundry, fill linen closets							
Karine	Clean balcony decks, tables, chairs, railing							
Karine	Take recycling and trash outside							
Patrick	Check for new reservations and respond							
Patrick	Replace guest keys							
Patrick	Answer phone calls							
Patrick	Refill pamphlets							

Weekly Schedule

Week of : _____

		Mon	Tues	Wed	Thu	Fri	Sat	Sun
Late Afternoon: 3:00 PM to 6:00 PM								
Paige	Help wherever needed							
Paige	Empty dishwasher							
Patrick	Check in guests, take payment, make index card							
Patrick	Take guests on tour of inn							
Patrick	Help with reservations, etc.							
Patrick	Post guests name in kitchen with food allergies							
Patrick	Check for new reservations and respond							
Patrick	Leave late arrival notes, if necessary							
Paige	Heat water, set up parlor with sugar, creamer, lemon wedges, cups, plates, etc.							
Paige	Serve beverages							
Alec	Cut and serve cakes							
Alec	Clean up snack area							

		Mon	Tues	Wed	Thu	Fri	Sat	Sun
Evening: 6:00 PM to 10:00 PM								
Alec	Load dishwasher							
Alec	Set up coffee pot for morning							
Alec	Prep kitchen for morning							
Alec	Post breakfast entrees on blackboard							
Paige	Check for new reservations and respond							
Paige	Leave late arrival notes, if necessary							
Paige	Close computer programs							
Alec	Adjust inside lights							
Alec	Turn on outside lights							
Alec	Lock front door, unless late arrival is expected							

		Mon	Tues	Wed	Thu	Fri	Sat	Sun
Outdoor: Weekly								
Alec	Put garbage cans out							
Alec	Put recycling out							
Chip	Cut grass and trim, weed beds, water lawn							
Chip	Spray for bugs							
Chip	Take trash to the dump							

		Mon	Tues	Wed	Thu	Fri	Sat	Sun
Deep Cleaning: Periodically								
Chip	Wash windows and balcony decks, as needed							
Chip	Paint touchups, as needed							
Chip	Clean carpets, annually							
Chip	Tighten hardware, as needed							
Chip	Clean fans and radiators, twice a year							
Chip	Clean appliances, grease traps and filters, every three to six months							
Chip	Check fire extinguishers and sprinkle system, annually							
Chip	Replace batteries in smoke detectors, annually							
Chip	Test emergency lighting, twice a year							
Karine	Wash curtains, as needed							
Karine	Flip and rotate mattresses, twice during high season							
Karine	Wash comforters, blankets, and pillow covers, every month							
Karine	Wash shower curtains, every month							
Karine	Clean baseboards, as needed							

After seeing what he and Paige were expected to do, Alec turned to his wife and asked, "Do you think we've bitten off more than we can chew?"

CHAPTER TWO

▼

"You're So Vain"
Words & Music by Carly Simon
Genre: Soft Rock, Released: November 1972

Sunday Afternoon—3rd of July

Paige was thrilled with the accommodations that her aunt had set aside for them. While she quickly unpacked their suitcases, Alec took a turn on the third-floor deck. He was able to walk the complete length of the inn and briefly listened to the conversation of a couple who was one deck below him. He suspected that they were the Pierces who Patrick had mentioned earlier. The fellow wanted to read a book and take a nap, and the woman agreed to let him as long as he promised to take her out later for a lobster dinner.

No one else was about and Alec gathered that guests mainly used the first and second floor balconies. Paige had changed into warmer clothes in their suite. It was a lot cooler in Maine than Alec had expected, and the weather had changed from partly cloudy to stormy. Now ready to have lunch and a nice long chat with her aunt, Paige took Alec's arm and said gaily, "Shall we?"

On the second-floor landing, the DunBartons ran into a stocky, middle-aged woman with dyed, bright red hair. With a Russian accent, she introduced herself as Karine Rybakov. Alec didn't need to be a great detective to guess her occupation. She was holding a cleaning bucket in one hand and a set of dirty linen in the other. As she dropped the sheets down a shoot in the sitting area and saw their bewildered expressions, Karine smiled. "It goes to the lower-level laundry room."

After chatting with the housekeeper, Alec and Paige recollected that Karine had been by Irena's side ever since the accident, not only doing the cleaning but also the cooking. Since her husband, a lobsterman, had been without her a whole week, Karine expressed her thanks to Alec and Paige for coming up to Maine on such short notice. Happy to return to her home and to her husband, Karine warmly embraced them.

The DunBartons wanted to know who was staying where but didn't detain her. They were well aware of how much she had to do to freshen up the rooms for current guests and prepare the rooms for new arrivals. Hoping to see her later, the couple continued to the first floor.

Patrick was at the desk and hailed them cheerfully. "It looks like it's going to storm. I turned on the gas fireplace. Miss Irena is in the kitchen heating up some cream of tomato soup and making grilled cheese sandwiches."

Paige immediately rushed into the kitchen to help her aunt. Irena was in command of the saucepan, so Paige took over the grill. In the meantime, Alec become familiar with where the plates, bowls, glasses, and cutlery were stored. By the time, the soup and sandwiches were ready, Alec had a table set by the double-sided fireplace.

Irena drew close to the table in her wheelchair and exclaimed, "It's so wonderful to have you both here! I've hated to put Karine out. She slept on the parlor couch outside my door. I'm afraid she snored, and I got little sleep. Nonetheless, she's been a Godsend, as you two are."

As they began to eat, Irena continued, "Besides having only half a body that works, the judge has been causing problems. He booked an entire month at the inn when he learned that his house had black mold." Less loudly, Irena swore, "He's like black mold, spreading his dark tentacles over everyone and everything."

Swallowing a crunchy piece of cheesy bread, "Alec inquired, "What's been going on?"

Irena stopped blowing on her spoonful of tomato soup to answer. "He talks about himself incessantly, belittles my other guests, takes up two spaces in the parking lot, drinks too much, and complains about the water pressure, the air conditioning, and the hardness of his bed. I've moved his room twice and worst of all, he said I nearly killed him yesterday!"

Alec couldn't imagine Paige's demure aunt even killing a bug.

Slowly, her story unfolded. The DunBartons learned that Aunt Irena always noted her guest's allergies and food preferences upon their arrival at the inn. She had been well aware of Judge Cassidy's allergy to bee venom. At teatime, she informed the judge that her Honey Spice Cake contained honey from Joan Bishop's bees. Instead of refraining from the treat, he took a large slice of the cake, swallowed one forkful, and had a terrible reaction.

Speaking quickly, Irena divulged, "It was pretty awful. His tongue swelled up and he was unable to breathe. Thank God, Dr. Pierce, his wife Leanne, and Hillary were here. Cassidy's blood pressure fell to a dangerous level. The judge was able to indicate to the doctor where he kept his EpiPen, and Alan Pierce injected the ephedrine into his right thigh.

"The doctor then drove Judge Cassidy to St. Andrew's Urgent Care Center. It's very close to the inn and the staff watched him till the evening. When he came back last night, he was as insolent as ever and threatened me."

"I didn't know that bee honey in a baked good could cause anaphylaxis," Paige responded. "It was hardly your fault."

"That's what Dr. Pierce said. He also told me that commercial honey is less likely to cause a reaction because it's heated and refined. The unprocessed honey from Joan's hives may have contained some pieces of a dead bee or a stinger containing venom. I'll be more aware of it in the future. The judge was told to go to

Lincoln Health Hospital if he has another encounter with a bee. Apparently, he's highly allergic."

While finishing their soup and sandwiches, Alec mulled over everything he'd heard and finally inquired, "When are we going to meet The Honorable Richard Cassidy?"

With clenched teeth, Irena replied, "Probably at afternoon tea. He never misses an opportunity to find something wrong with my cakes."

Over the next two hours, Aunt Irena gave Alec a crash course on how to make gluten-free Chocolate Chip Dream Bars, Sunday's tea cake. She taught him how to cut the butter into a dry flour mixture with a pastry blender and explained why gluten-free almond flour was more difficult to work with than ordinary all-purpose wheat flour.

Alec not only enjoyed the precise way he was told to measure the ingredients but also how wonderful the cakelike bar cookies smelled in the oven. He even became proficient at whisking away dirty utensils and at putting away unused foodstuffs in the pantry and refrigerator.

When Alec swallowed the last few semisweet chocolate morsels from the bag, Irena showed Alec where she kept the grocery list and how to add to it. While Alec was discovering how to make his first afternoon tea snack, Paige sat with Patrick at the front desk to learn the proper way to answer the phone, greet guests, and check the computer property management system for new online reservations.

At a quarter to four, Paige, Irena, and Alec readied the first-floor parlor for afternoon tea. Paige was told to bring out from the kitchen a pitcher of milk, cut lemons, a bowl of sugar, and a tea kettle filled with boiling hot water. Irena removed a wooden box of assorted tea bags from the parlor sideboard. And Alec was instructed to cut the dream bars, into 3-inch by 1-inch slices and place them on a platter.

Alec was amazed at how the quiet inn's parlor became a center of activity within ten minutes. Patrick emerged from behind the front desk, Dr. Pierce and Leanne came in from the balcony, and a sexy middle-aged woman bustled through the foyer door with two large shopping bags. Another woman, less attractive but nevertheless interesting looking, followed in her wake.

Irena introduced her niece and Alec to the newcomers and presented them, in turn—Dr. Alan Pierce and his wife Leanne, Hillary Fairchild, and Joan Bishop. It took Alec a few moments to memorize everyone's features and attributes.

Alan was in his late sixties, approachable, easy going, and a great listener. Those were valuable assets for a general practitioner to have. Leanne appeared to be several years younger, blonde, and wore huge glasses that made her look like Annie Hall.

Hillary was a breath of fresh air. Her dark, shoulder-length hair moved every time she spoke. She had a lovely British accent, and her catlike eyes were alert, as if waiting for a tasty mouse to run across her path.

The other woman, Patrick's mother, was attractive in her own way. Even though her hair was less glossy than Hillary's, her exaggerated facial expressions and twangy voice made her equally unforgettable.

Everyone wanted to know how the judge was feeling after his encounter with the near-deadly bee honey. Since there was also honey in the Chocolate Chip Dream Bars, Irena wisely thawed out some pecan pie for Richard Cassidy. It had been prepared with less dangerous light corn syrup.

Thirty minutes later, the judge showed up. Wearing well-pressed grey slacks and a peach-colored cashmere sweater, he walked into the room from the inside staircase and asked in a charming manner, "Were you talking about me?"

Alec had expected him to be different—unkempt or overweight. Instead, Richard Cassidy was dapper, sporting a pencil thin mustache that was darker than his light brown hair. Most arresting were his steel blue eyes and silky, well-modulated voice.

The judge didn't stay long. He shook Alec's hand and winked at Paige before taking a cup of Earl Grey tea and a slice of pecan pie. Gazing at Irena and Joan, he uttered, "I trust you both have given up on killing me."

Patrick snarled, "Leave my mother alone."

Nodding, Richard Cassidy took his snack up the stairs and said, "With pleasure."

Alec felt like laughing but held his mirth inside. It was Joan who responded and simply said, "He's so vain."

That was all Alec had to hear before belting out,

> You walked into the party like you were walking onto a yacht
> Your hat strategically dipped below one eye
> Your scarf it was apricot
>
> You had one eye in the mirror as you watched yourself gavotte
> And all the girls dreamed that they'd be your partner
> They'd be your partner, and...
>
> You're so vain, you probably think this song is about you
> You're so vain, I'll bet you think this song is about you
> Don't you? Don't you?
>
> You had me several years ago when I was still quite naive
> When you said that we made such a pretty pair
> And that you would never leave
>
> But you gave away the things you loved and one of them was me
> I had some dreams; they were clouds in my coffee
> Clouds in my coffee
> Clouds in my coffee

The mood in the room returned to normal after Alec finished the first half of the song. The only one who remained quiet was Joan Bishop.

It was not until Alec and Irena were clearing away the afternoon tea accompaniments that Irena revealed, "Patrick is

Richard Cassidy's son. Eighteen years ago, Joan had a fling with Dick. He was a lawyer then, working for the district attorney. They never married and he paid her a lump sum custodial payment in lieu of monthly child support. He never wanted to have anything to do with Patrick. It's such a shame."

Alec had to agree.

The DunBartons had a quiet evening with Aunt Irena. At five, Karine, the housekeeper, hurried off to see her husband and promised to return at ten in the morning. Joan left minutes after her and came back at 7:00 o'clock with a salad and a casserole containing chicken thighs, almond rice, and mango salsa. Together the Bishops departed, leaving Alec, Paige, and Irena to have a pleasant dinner in the breakfast room.

The inn's guests were out for the evening. The Pierces set off for a pricey lobster restaurant with Hillary Fairchild in tow. Upon learning that Hillary was a home decorator, Leanne invited her to join them. Both women loved to shop and decided to go antiquing the following day.

Guests staying in Portside Retreat had an early flight and were in for the night. That left, Richard Cassidy. Thankfully, he had made himself scarce.

After dinner, Paige settled her aunt in her ground floor suite. Irena was tucked in bed when Paige joined Alec in Mariner's Retreat. The night was cold and clear, and Alec induced his wife to step outside to see the stars. Alec wrapped his arms around Paige's waist and asked, "Are you very tired?"

Paige looked up at him. "A bit, but nothing a hot bath can't cure. Alec hustled Paige back into the room when she shivered and remarked, "Let's get you into that whirlpool tub."

The bathroom was appointed with fluffy white towels, comfy his and her robes, and a basket of fragrant gels, shampoos, and hair conditioners. Paige poured the bath gel into the cascading hot water, removed her clothes, and slipped into the foamy water."

After resting her head against a rolled-up towel, Paige smiled up at Alec. "Sit down on the edge of the tub and talk to me. What do you think of the other guests? And that judge? He appears to be an unsavory character."

Alec concurred. "I'm afraid you're right. But let's talk about something more pleasant. Tomorrow is Independence Day. In the evening, the townspeople are going to shoot off fireworks over the harbor to celebrate the fourth. Your aunt usually invites a few people over to watch the display from the inn's first-floor deck.

"In the morning, Irena is also going to see off the couple that has to leave early, so we don't have to get up until 7:30 AM to make breakfast. After I finish my chores, Irena said we should take the afternoon off to see the town. It's going to be warm and sunny."

"That will be nice," Paige sighed. "It's been about ten years since I last visited Boothbay Harbor. I hope you don't mind spending five weeks of our two-month vacation working at the inn."

Alec shook his head. "Not at all. You know I love to cook, and Irena has already given me a lot of great tips. No, Lass, just relax. We're going to have fun helping your aunt run her bed and breakfast."

CHAPTER THREE

▼

"A Beautiful Morning"
Words & Music by Felix Cavaliere and Eddie Brigati
Genre: Pop Rock, Released: March 1968

Monday Morning—4th of July

Alec was finished with his morning chores by 11:00 o'clock. For breakfast, he and Irena heated up brown and serve sausages, made a Spinach Frittata, and prepared Waffles with Strawberries and Cream. Since Irena had Banana Walnut Bread in the freezer, Alec just had to thaw the loaf and slice it. Paige served everyone on the first-floor deck like an experienced waitress.

Earlier, Irena had arranged baskets for each of the guest tables that were filled with creamers, sugar, sugar substitutes, butter, jams, syrups, napkins, and utensils, so it was easy for Paige to bring over all the extras in one trip. Cleanup was a cinch and everyone, but the judge arrived between nine and ten.

Ten minutes past ten, after the posted breakfast time, the Honorable Richard Cassidy wandered into the kitchen without saying a word. He smelled of alcohol and poured a hefty amount of liquid from a metal flask into a glass of tomato juice. Alec suspected it was vodka. Cassidy stayed long enough to finish his drink and gather up a few slices of banana bread in a napkin.

When he departed, Irena warned Alec, "The man is terribly rude and just took the remainder of our banana bread. You'll have to make some more next Monday. After hearing that he was also expected to prepare a baked good every day for breakfast along with an afternoon teacake, Alec wasn't sure which statement was more worrying."

Alec had nothing to fear. Irena gave him concise instructions on how to make the yeast dough for Karine's Cinnamon Babka. After he placed the dough into the kitchen's warming drawer to rise, Irena had him prepare the cinnamon nut mixture that Karine planned to add to the dough before baking it. Although Alec would have liked to see the housekeeper finish *his* masterpiece, Irena laughed and promised, "You'll get a chance to make four or five more while you're here."

Before shooing the DunBartons out of the kitchen, she reminded, "Afternoon tea is at four. Today is going to be a slow day. A nice young couple is going to arrive later this afternoon from St. Paul, Minnesota, and will be staying for three nights in Portside Retreat. They've been here before, so I don't expect too much excitement. Have a good time in town."

Paige took a moment to run upstairs to gather a few things together. When she returned with a bulging tote bag, Alec took it from her and complained, "What in the world did you pack? We're only going out for a few hours."

Winking, Paige replied, "It's pretty sunny outside and I thought we should bring sunscreen, bug spray, sun hats, our phones, a bottle of water, and my sweater."

While exiting the front door of the inn, Alec agreed, "The weather is gorgeous," and then sang out,

It's a beautiful morning, ah
I think I'll go outside for a while
And just smile
Just take in some clean fresh air, boy
No sense in staying inside

If the weather's fine and you've got the time
It's your chance to wake up and plan another brand-new day
Either way

It's a beautiful morning, ah
Each bird keeps singing his own song
So long
I've got to be on my way now
No fun just hanging around
I got to cover ground
You couldn't keep me down
It just ain't no good if the sun shines
When you're still inside
Shouldn't hide
Still inside
Shouldn't hide
Still inside, shouldn't hide

There will be children with robins and flowers
Sunshine caresses each new waking hour

Seems to me that people keep seeing more and more each day
Gotta say, lead the way
It's okay, brand-new day
Gotta say, it's okay
Brand new day, gotta say, lead the way

Energized by the lyrics, Alec took Paige's arm and headed to the center of town, which was a short five-minute walk from the inn. Along the way, they saw quaint gift shops, clothes stores, art galleries, and restaurants.

Since it was Independence Day, many of the businesses were decorated with red, white, and blue streamers. The street was filled with sightseers, wheeling their children in strollers. Alec imagined that most of them were eagerly anticipating the fireworks display later in the evening.

After talking to the parents of a child with fading face paint on his cheeks, Alec learned that the family had been to the Railway Village Museum the previous day for one of the Boothbay Harbor

Windjammer Events. Earnestly, the boy warned, "Even though it's not free today, you must see the choo-choo train."

Paige promised they would as they continued down the street. When the DunBartons neared the Boothbay Harbor Footbridge, which was suspended over shimmering blue water, Paige recalled, "This is one of the town's landmarks. The bridge was built in 1901 to connect the east and west sides of the harbor."

Together the couple walked to the middle of the 885-foot-long span to take pictures. Alec grew excited as he pointed to the Land's End Inn and exclaimed, "I can see it from here. It looks beautiful even with the tide going out. I'm glad the tide shifts every six hours. It won't be long before the harbor fills up again."

There were signs along the street called, "The Museum in the Streets," denoting other points of interest. Too hungry to thoroughly read them, Alec suggested, "Let's find a nice place to have lunch."

Alec and Paige looked at several menus that were posted along the pier. When they stopped to pick up boat trip brochures from a kiosk, they heard live music coming from the Fisherman's Wharf Inn. The couple quickly found seats in the casual eatery that faced the bay and listened to two musicians perform their own tunes and songs by Jimmy Buffet.

Tapping his feet to the music, Alec perused the menu and quickly decided upon a Guinness Braised Corned Beef Reuben with a beer. Paige had a bit more difficulty choosing a meal and finally settled on a Panko Fried Haddock Sandwich and a pink lemonade. The service was great and the food wonderful. Alec and Paige eventually pulled themselves away from the eatery to search for a nearby liquor store.

The DunBartons were not disappointed. On Commercial Street, they found a small food market that had Glenlivet 12 on the shelf. Concerned he was going to overpay for his favorite treat, Alec eyed the fellow behind the register and asked, "How much more expensive is your liquor from those in budget priced stores?"

Curtly, the man announced, "All liquor in Maine is price fixed. You may get a dollar or two off at a supermarket if the store is running a weekly sale."

Alec was thrilled, glad he didn't have to borrow Irena's car to go to Hannaford's Market. After purchasing two bottles, the duo stopped off at a few more stores to see what kind of merchandise they offered.

Paige and Alec returned to the inn at 3:30 PM, ready for hot tea and Karine's Cinnamon Babka. After greeting Patrick, who had the script for *The Importance of Being Earnest* in front of him, Alec followed his nose to the kitchen where Karine was setting her cake on a cooling rack.

With a worried expression, she voiced, "I hope it has enough time to cool. If we try to cut into it while it's warm, the buttery cinnamon nut mixture may tumble out from the folded layers."

Alec, now equally concerned, replied. "Let's wait till the last minute to cut it open. Have the other guests returned from their outings?"

While Karine set a bowl of cut lemons on the kitchen island, she enumerated, "Your aunt and Joan are going over the week's income and expenses. Joan is a top-notch bookkeeper and does the yearly taxes too.

"As to the others, Dr. Pierce is nursing a bee sting on his hand. I told him not to swat at Joan's bees. They're a feisty bunch but make wonderful honey. The ladies, Leanne and Hillary haven't returned from their shopping excursion yet, and the judge went to his house to inspect how the mold removal is going. God help the workmen if it's not up to his standards!"

Alec stayed to help the housekeeper. When he and Karine entered the parlor with the tea paraphernalia and uncut cake, Alec found his wife sitting beside Patrick. Paige was reciting,

Paige as Jack: *Oh, pleasure, pleasure! What else should bring one anywhere? Eating as usual, I see, Algy!*

Patrick as Algernon: *[Stiffly.] I believe it is customary in good society to take some slight refreshment at five o'clock. Where have you been since last Thursday?*

Paige as Jack: *[Sitting down on the sofa.] In the country.*

Patrick as Algernon: *What on earth do you do there?*

Paige as Jack: *[Pulling off his gloves.] When one is in town one amuses oneself. When one is in the country one amuses other people. It is excessively boring.*

Patrick as Algernon: *And who are the people you amuse?*

Paige as Jack: [Airily.] *Oh, neighbors, neighbors.*

Patrick as Algernon: *Got nice neighbors in your part of Shropshire?*

Paige as Jack: *Perfectly horrid! Never speak to one of them.*

Patrick as Algernon: *How immensely you must amuse them! [Goes over and takes sandwich.] By the way, Shropshire is your county, is it not?*

Paige as Jack: *Eh? Shropshire? Yes, of course. Hallo! Why all these cups? Why cucumber sandwiches? Why such reckless extravagance in one so young? Who is coming to tea?*

Patrick as Algernon: *Oh! merely Aunt Augusta and Gwendolen.*

Paige as Jack: *How perfectly delightful!*

Patrick as Algernon: *Yes, that is all very well; but I am afraid Aunt Augusta won't quite approve of your being here.*

Alec watched Paige in fascination. She had done a few lines in *The Crook and the Contessa*, a movie that was being filmed during their honeymoon but had forgotten how natural she was. As she responded to Patrick playing the part of Algernon, she made hand movements to simulate the action.

When the pair stopped saying their lines, Irena and Joan, who had just entered the room, called, "Bravo, Encore!"

Patrick rose to his feet and pulled Paige up from the couch. Together, they bowed in unison.

The doctor was the only one to join them at teatime. The swelling on his hand had gone down with the aid of an ice pack that Karine had given him. Joan apologized for the discomfort that her bees had caused him, but the doctor graciously admitted, "I should have known better."

Teatime was extremely pleasant. Dr. Pierce shared stories of how some of his patients had come to be stung by insects and bitten by animals. Patrick told the others how he planned to go to Emerson College in Boston for a Drama and Theater Arts Degree. The only thing dampening his dream was the cost of tuition and housing.

With a crooked smile, Joan added, "I hope to get some money from his father." Joan looked toward the front door to make sure the judge wasn't standing there and explained. "Dick thought he was being clever when he gave me a lump sum to bring Patrick up.

"However, I met with a child support lawyer last week. Even though Patrick just turned eighteen, I learned that old custodial payments can be overturned under the Doctrine of Changed Circumstances. That's when the supporting parent has gotten a better job with more pay over the years."

Softly, Irena agreed, "You're very clever, dear. If anyone can get money out of him, it's you."

Dr. Pierce complemented Patrick on his choice of college and mentioned that Leanne had a hard time when their three children left home for school. Sipping Earl Grey tea, he added, "Leanne has been showing an interest in interior design and had great taste when she updated our home in Bennington with new fabrics and furnishings. I'm glad my wife and Hillary Fairchild went out for the day. Do you know if Hillary has a successful business?"

Joan replied, "Hillary is quite famous and has a retail store in New York City. Yesterday, she told me that she's tired of redecorating houses and is rather lonely. She and her husband divorced five years ago, and her son recently married and moved to Connecticut."

Gazing at everyone, Paige remarked, "I can see why my aunt likes running a bed and breakfast. You meet interesting people and get to renew friendships with people who come back year after year."

Besides enjoying the comradery, Alec unashamedly took two large pieces of the babka and then complained that he might not be hungry for dinner. Since Irena just planned to order pizza for the three of them, they decided to have it delivered when Alec's appetite returned.

After the doctor retired to his room to finish his book, Karine and Joan cleared away the dishes to give Paige, Alec, and Irena an opportunity to talk, sit in the sun, and watch the tide come in.

CHAPTER FOUR

▼

"Wooden Ships"
Words & Music by Paul Kanter,
Steven Stills, and David Crosby
Genre: Soft Rock, Released: April 1969

Monday Evening—4th of July

At dusk, the first-floor balcony began to fill up with Irena's neighbors and the inn's guests to view the July 4th fireworks. From the deck, Alec watched the boats in the harbor maneuver themselves to find the best place to observe the upcoming show. To make the evening more memorable, Karine set out a pitcher of pink lemonade along with chips and spinach dip.

The first to arrive were the Bishops, followed by Chip Granger, the town's handyman. Even though, Chip was probably in his mid-forties, he was dressed like a teenager, wearing a baseball cap backwards. He removed his hat when Irena introduced him to Alec and Paige. His long, dirty-blonde hair came tumbling out, and he proudly flung it back to show off his mane.

Joan Bishop engaged him in conversation, reminding him that he promised to weed her garden on Thursday. Chip responded, "Sure thing," while eyeing Paige with interest.

Instead of warning the handyman with an offhand remark, Alec welcomed the Pierces and Hillary who had just joined them. On the way back from their shopping spree, the ladies had stopped off for a pleasant dinner. Alan Pierce was as laid back as usual and said to Alec, "I'm thrilled Leanne has made a new friend. I'm a stick in the mud when it comes to shopping."

Patrick informed the group that the young couple staying in the Portside Suite were dining in town and planned to watch the fireworks from the harbor. That left only Richard Cassidy. He made his entrance a few minutes later. He was quite pleasant to the DunBartons, asking about their day and making suggestions about places they should visit.

To Alec, he seemed standoffish with Hillary and was amazed to hear that the judge had hired her to redecorate his home the year before. They had gotten to know each other when she had stayed at Irena's the previous fall.

Richard was less civil upon seeing Chip Granger. In a curt tone, he remarked, "I'm surprised to see you here. Don't you usually watch the fireworks from your neighborhood bar. Your buddies are no doubt, going to miss you."

Chip chuckled. "Unlike you, I have friends."

Not letting the matter drop, the judge threatened, "We'll see how many friends you have when I sue you in court."

Patrick interrupted their squabble by announcing, "I think the fireworks are about to start."

Chip helped himself to lemonade while Joan said in a low voice to Richard, "Why do you always malign people and make them feel like two cents? You know the mold wasn't his fault. He installed your new washing machine after your last one leaked. You should have checked for damage then."

In response, Richard gazed at his son who was speaking to Karine and stated, "Don't expect me to give you any money for his acting school. He's never going to amount to much, and I'm sure the family court magistrate is going to side with me!"

The fireworks began exactly at 9:00 o'clock. Irena had Paige turn off the balcony's ceiling lights. The evening was cool, and the sky was a velvety black. Everyone grouped together in the corner of the balcony to get the best view. The show was mesmerizing and there were oohs and aahs from the onlookers as flashes of blue, red, and silver streaked and exploded above the harbor.

At first, Alec wasn't sure he heard someone cry out in pain. It wasn't until there was a slight lull in the display that Alec saw Richard Cassidy hunched over against the railing.

Quickly he turned on the lights while Patrick complained, "You're going to ruin the … show." He finished the sentence as Alec rushed to the judge and asked, "Are you okay?"

With his eyes bulging and tongue swelling, Cassidy managed to utter, 'Damn bee!" before passing out.

Dr. Pierce went into action after locating the judge's EpiPen, which was in Cassidy's windbreaker pocket. The others laid the collapsed judge on the deck as the doctor plunged the auto injector of epinephrine into Cassidy's thigh. As he massaged the area for ten seconds, he yelled to Leanne to get his medical bag and for someone else to call 911.

Patrick took the initiative to call an ambulance as Leanne ran up the stairs to retrieve her husband's medical kit from their suite. Alan checked his patient's pulse and heart, and then searched the judge's body for the presence of a bee's stinger, expressing hope that it was no longer attached.

Upon rechecking his vital signs, he murmured, "His condition is worsening. If the ambulance doesn't get here in another five minutes, I'm going to inject him with a second dose of epinephrine. His breathing is labored, and he's having a severe anaphylactic reaction."

While waiting, the doctor tilted the judge's head back to further open his airway. More alarmed, Dr. Pierce pulled an EpiPen from the medical bag that Leanne had retrieved. After checking the dosage, he injected Cassidy a second time, and told Patrick to let the EMS personnel into the inn as soon as they arrive.

The next five minutes was a blur. While Pierce was doing CPR on Cassidy, the emergency workers entered the inn. They quickly placed him on a stretcher, attached oxygen, and rushed him to the ambulance. Dr. Pierce was steps behind the EMS team. The fireworks show ended moments later with a final loud and colorful display.

Chip was the first to comment, "He didn't look good. Can a person die from a bee sting?"

Joan cried, "Can they hold me responsible? My bees usually settle in after dark. The evening was really clear. I wonder if they reacted to the firework's smoke and noise vibrations more than usual?"

Patrick heard his mother's remark upon returning to the first-floor balcony and pleaded, "Please don't blame yourself, mom. The ambulance just took off."

Directing his attention to Leanne, he added, "Your husband is following them in your car and will let us know how the judge is doing once he gets to Lincoln Health Hospital."

Hillary, who had been quiet till then, muttered to herself, while Irena offered, "I think we may need something stronger to drink than lemonade."

While Karine was wheeling the bar cart over from the kitchen, Alec gathered up the dead bee and the two empty EpiPens in a handkerchief and stuffed them in his pocket. The cart contained an assortment of liquors, spritzers, and a bottle of red wine.

Since there wasn't a single-malt scotch among the liquors, Paige fetched one of Alec's bottles from their third-floor suite. Alec was very annoyed to see Chip top up his half-filled glass of lemonade with *his* single-malt Glenlivet.

The ladies—Paige, Hillary, and Leanne opted for the red wine, and Karine returned to the kitchen to make hot rum toddies for herself and Irena. When everyone was served, they took seats around a table and began to talk.

Despite the cool evening temperatures, no one seemed ready to turn in. With the help of cozy warm throws and buttoned up jackets, the group remained outside drinking and wondering about Richard Cassidy's fate.

While watching the lighted wooden ships head back to the harbor for the night, Alec began to sing softly,

If you smile at me, I will understand
'Cause that is something
Everybody everywhere does in the same language

I can see by your coat, my friend
You're from the other side
There's just one thing I got to know
Can you tell me please, who won?

Say, can I have some of your purple berries?
Yes, I've been eating them for six or seven weeks now
Haven't got sick once
Probably keep us both alive

Wooden ships on the water, very free and easy
Easy, you know the way it's supposed to be
Silver people on the shoreline, let us be
Talkin' 'bout very free and easy

Horror grips us as we watch you die
All we can do is echo your anguished cries
Stare as all human feelings die
We are leaving, you don't need us

Go, take your sister then, by the hand
Lead her away from this foreign land
Far away, where we might laugh again
We are leaving, you don't need us

And it's a fair wind blowin' warm
Out of the south over my shoulder
Guess I'll set a course and go

Paige was about to tell the ladies and Chip to ignore her husband when Hillary asked, "Do you think he's dead?"

Although he felt sure the judge had met his maker, Alec said assuredly, "The doctors at the hospital will pull him through."

As soon as he uttered those words, the front doorbell rang. Patrick quickly answered it and came back to the group with Walt Taylor, chief of the Boothbay Harbor Police Department.

Alec studied the man for a few seconds. He appeared to be in his mid-fifties and was about six feet two inches tall. The grey hair at his temples and his stubbly chin made his face look rugged.

Holding the hot toddy with both hands, Irena cried, "He died, didn't he?"

The chief looked at the faces of those assembled and confirmed in a gruff voice, "Judge Cassidy passed away in the Emergency Room of the hospital. All sudden deaths in Maine have to be investigated. I need to get statements from the guests who saw the 'accident' and plan to leave tomorrow morning."

Alec introduced himself and Paige to the policeman saying, "We'll be here until the beginning of August. My wife, Paige, and I are helping Irena run the inn while she's recuperating from her accident."

Both Leanne and Hillary also acknowledged that they were going to be in town for a week. Since the Bishops, Chip, and Karine were residents and the inn's guests weren't going anywhere for a while, Walt drew up a chair and said, "I won't keep you then. Just tell me what happened, and I'll return in the morning to get your individual statements."

Alec answered for the group and told the officer what took place during the fireworks display. While the police chief was jotting down notes, Dr. Pierce returned from the hospital. He had to remain behind to answer medical questions posed by the emergency staff.

Walt also questioned the doctor and wrote down what he said. Shortly later, he rose from his seat and thanked everyone for their help. As he was about to leave, he asked, "What did you do with the EpiPens?"

Smiling, Alec pulled the handkerchief from his pocket and handed it to the chief. Walt gazed at Alec as if seeing him for the first time and remarked, "You know police procedure."

While escorting him out of the inn, Alec informed him that he had taken part in several suspicious death investigations while serving on Flagship Cruise Line as its controller and the liaison between the ship and the Fort Lauderdale Police Department.

It was 11:00 o'clock when Alec returned to the balcony. Upon learning from Paige that Karine had helped her aunt get ready for bed and the others had gone home or to their suites. Alec suggested, "Let's take the beverage cart back to the kitchen now and clean up tomorrow."

Despite the late hour, Alec and Paige found it difficult to relax, and they stepped onto their private balcony, dressed in warm robes. With a nightcap in his hand, Alec asked, "What did you think of Chief of Police Taylor?"

Wickedly, Paige answered, "He's a very sexy looking man."

Not sure he posed the right question, Alec acknowledged, "You're not the only woman who seemed susceptible to his charms. Hillary wasn't able to take her eyes off him."

Paige agreed. "Since I have you, I'll let Hillary have him."

When Alec finished off his whisky, Paige whispered in his ear, "Let's go inside. I know something that may induce us to sleep."

Guessing what was on his wife's mind, the couple turned off the lights, removed their robes, and got into bed. Moments later, all thoughts of the police chief's investigation disappeared from Alec's mind.

CHAPTER FIVE

▼

"Dust In The Wind"
Words & Music Kerry Livgren
Genre: Soft Rock, Released: January 1978

Tuesday Morning—5th of July

Even though Alec and Paige had less than eight hours of sleep, they both woke up feeling refreshed and ready to make breakfast for the inn's guests. After taking quick showers, the couple entered the kitchen to find Irena still in her nightdress. She had all the ingredients for the meals set out on the prep island.

Irena looked as though she'd had a sleepless night and moaned, "I couldn't stay in bed another minute worrying about my inn's reputation. Do you think our guests will be hungry?"

Alec glanced at the Land's End Weekly Menu. It read:

	Juice	Meat	Savory Dish	Sweet Dish	Baked Good	Afternoon Tea Cake
Sun	Orange Apple V8	Pork or Turkey Sausage	Swiss and Mushroom Quiche	Blintz Souffle w. Blueberries	Date Nut Loaves	Chocolate Chip Dream Bars

	Juice	Meat	Savory Dish	Sweet Dish	Baked Good	Afternoon Tea Cake
Mon	Orange Cranberry Tomato	Pork or Turkey Sausage	Spinach Frittata	Waffles w. Strawberries and Cream	Banana Walnut Bread	Cinnamon Babka
Tue	Orange Prune V8	Bacon or Canadian Bacon	Egg Scrambler w. Cheese, Mushrooms & Asparagus	Baked Apple French Toast	Scones with Jam and Cream	Almond Slices
Wed	Orange Apple Tomato	Pork or Turkey Sausage	Ham and Cheese Parcel	Blueberry Buttermilk Pancakes	Pumpkin Cranberry Loaves	Sour Cream Coffee Cake
Thu	Orange Cranberry V8	Bacon or Canadian Bacon	Bacon Quiche in Hash Brown Crust	Blintz Souffle with Cherries	Cinnamon Crescent Rolls	Peach or Apple Turnovers
Fri	Orange Prune Tomato	Pork or Turkey Sausage	Broccoli Frittata	Waffles with Peaches and Cream	Patrick's Irish Soda Bread	Pecan Pie Squares
Sat	Orange Cranberry V8	Bacon or Canadian Bacon	Egg Scrambler w. Smoked Salmon and Scallions	Banana Wholewheat Pancakes	Cheese Danish	Honey Spice Cake

Glad that Irena had started to get the ingredients together for the extensive Tuesday menu, Alec began to snap the ends of the asparagus off while Paige washed and finely sliced the apples. Aunt Irena was able to give them clear and concise instructions while she masterfully combined the ingredients for the scones with just her right hand.

Meal preparation took forty-five minutes and the Baked Apple French Toast had just come out of the oven when the Pierces arrived for breakfast. Since it was lightly raining outside, they headed to a table in the breakfast room where Paige brought them two cups of piping hot coffee.

The couple was unsure what to have. Leanne was concerned about gaining too much weight while in Maine and decided to choose one item. Even though Irena's scones were richer and a bit sweeter than a Scottish scone, Alec recommended them, and she gladly agreed. When Dr. Pierce asked for a plain scrambled egg, Alec was reminded of his good friend on the Pegasus, Dr. Abbot. It was curious how the two men seemed to gravitate to simple and plain food.

Hillary appeared soon after and had the baked French toast with bacon. When the couple from St. Paul, Minnesota, showed up, Irena introduced them to the others and took their order. They too choose the French toast but were more interested in hearing what had happened to the man who was stung by the bee.

It didn't take long before everyone was talking about the judge and his misadventure. Alan Pierce was the most restrained and remarked, "I'm not surprised he had a severe reaction. If a drop of honey in a spice cake could cause him to go into anaphylaxis, he had to be highly allergic to bee venom."

Leanne looked over at Hillary before announcing, "He wasn't a very nice man. I spoke to him the other day and he looked bored and yawned the whole time. I don't think anyone is going to miss him."

"I dated him for a month last year," Hillary divulged. "It was the biggest mistake of my life!"

Alec appeared from inside the kitchen and asked, "How did you meet him?"

Sipping her tea, Hillary explained, "We met while I was antique shopping, and he asked me to redecorate his beautiful home on the bay. I only agreed to date him after my project was finished and I was paid. I never mix business with pleasure."

Irena chimed, "Very smart, dear."

Hillary continued, "Dick was not only a narcissist but also very controlling. I actually started to fear him. I changed my standing reservation from September to July just to avoid him.

"When we first met, he was engaging. But it didn't last long. He started to belittle me in small ways and discount my views. He liked to show me off but wasn't interested in me as a person. I finally told him to buzz off after he arrived late for a dinner date with a ridiculous excuse.

"Unfortunately, that wasn't the end of it. When I returned to New York City, he pestered me with unwanted phone calls, texts, and emails. I ended up calling the police chief in Boothbay Harbor to see if he could do something."

Alec smiled, "Did Walt Taylor put a stop to his annoying advances?"

Hillary, looking like a cat that swallowed a canary, responded, "It did the trick. I just wish I had known then that the police chief was so ruggedly handsome. I would have thanked him for looking into the matter when I first arrived in town and also let him know that Richard had booked a room at Land's End prior to my arrival."

The conversation ended when Patrick came into the breakfast room for some coffee before taking his place at the front desk. Alec found himself wondering whether the young man was the judge's only living relative and stood to inherit.

While Paige cleared the tables and filled the dishwasher, Alec baked the Almond Slices for afternoon tea. Even though Alec had finished off the French toast for his breakfast, he hungrily ingested several warm almond tea cookies that were cooling on a wire rack. They were full of nuts, chocolate chips, and craisins. He found them richer and softer than its cousin—almond biscotti.

Free for the rest of the morning and most of the afternoon, Alec and Paige joined Patrick in the parlor to find out what the other guests were up to. The young man was practicing his lines with Leanne and stopped a moment to tell them that Walt Taylor was interviewing Dr. Pierce. Since the rain had stopped and the sun was out, the police chief had decided to take the doctor's statement on the first-floor balcony.

Alec took a seat on the sofa closest to the open balcony door but was unable to hear the men's conversation. Chuckling, Paige teased, "You can't eavesdrop on them, can you?"

Aware that his wife knew him too well, he ignored Paige and asked Patrick, "When did the chief arrive?"

Leanne answered for him, "A few minutes ago. He wants to speak to everyone who witnessed the judge's death. That horrible man was here one day and gone the next."

Her observation brought a song to mind, and Alec sang out,

I close my eyes
Only for a moment, and the moment's gone
All my dreams
Pass before my eyes, a curiosity

Dust in the wind
All they are is dust in the wind

Same old song
Just a drop of water in an endless sea
All we do
Crumbles to the ground, though we refuse to see

Dust in the wind
All we are is dust in the wind

Now don't hang on
Nothing lasts forever but the earth and sky
It slips away
And all your money won't another minute buy

Dust in the wind
All we are is dust in the wind
(All we are is dust in the wind)
Dust in the wind
(Everything is dust in the wind)
Everything is dust in the wind
(In the wind)

The police chief entered the parlor as Alec finished the song and commented, "Very apt. As he escorted Leanne Pierce outdoors, he added, "I'd like to speak to you and your wife after I take Mrs. Pierce's statement. Please remain here until I'm ready for you."

Alec acknowledged that they would be available and said to Patrick, "This must be awkward for you. When did you learn that Judge Cassidy was your father?"

Patrick grimaced. "About nine months ago. My mother told me when I applied for college in Boston. She hoped to get some money from him to help pay the tuition. Up until then, she let me think that my dad had died when I was an infant. I could see it was a sore subject with her while I was growing up, and my mother's brother was like a father to me. He's the one who got me interested in acting."

Alec couldn't help asking, "Do you know whether your father had a will?"

Paige glanced at Alec with an expression that said, "You're overstepping your bounds, mister," while Patrick shook his head.

Several moments later, Patrick responded, "My mother thinks I was his only living relative and doubts he ever wrote a will."

Although a bee was responsible for Cassidy's death, Alec wondered whether beekeepers could induce their little honey makers to kill.

Alec was called next by Walt Taylor to give his statement. The police chief took down his words with a digital voice recorder and referred to a list of questions from a pocket notebook. Alec's observations about the previous night tallied with the Pierces.

Moving from his standard questions, the chief asked, "Why did you collect the two empty EpiPens and the dead bee? That was an unusual thing for you to do."

Smiling, Alec recapped, "After solving several murders for my cruise line and working with the police in Fort Lauderdale, Las Vegas, and the Northern Constabulary in Scotland, I've learned how to collect evidence at a 'crime' scene."

Walt accepted his statement and resumed, "I checked out all the inn's guests for police records when I returned to my office last night. I also had a very pleasant conversation with Dan McGill in the Fort Lauderdale Homicide Department. He told me that I can rely on your instincts even though you often break into song to describe your suspects and to decipher clues."

Now completely serious, Taylor asked, "Do you think the judge was murdered?"

Alec was unable to answer him directly and merely offered, "Cassidy was a narcissist, had a sizable estate, and used his office to bully people. He was a prime candidate to be murdered. That said, I can't see how it was done."

After Walt concurred, he added, "I sent his corpse to OCME, the Office of the Chief Medical Examiner, in Augusta, Maine. The department is responsible for reviewing witness statements, examining the "crime" scene, collecting medical and pharmacy records, running toxicological tests, and if necessary, conducting autopsies.

"It's done whenever there is a sudden death. Approximately three thousand deaths are reported every year in Maine and about thirteen hundred cases are investigated by the OCME when cause of death cannot be determined. This case appears to be open and shut, but you never know.

"In the meantime, can you keep your eyes open? As you said, Judge Cassidy was not a likable person."

CHAPTER SIX

▼

"Maneater"

Words & Music by Sara Allen, Daryl Hall, and John Oates
Genre: Soft Rock, Released: October 1982

Tuesday Afternoon—5th of July

Alec, Paige, and Aunt Irena shared their opinions of Police Chief Taylor over a meal of tuna fish salad and potato chips. Alec didn't mind having simple lunches since they were sandwiched between lavish breakfasts and delicious afternoon tea cakes.

When Paige was interviewed by the officer, she boasted about Alec's ability to read people and solve puzzles. Irena let Walt know how the judge had behaved while staying at the inn. She was also present when Chief Taylor searched Richard Cassidy's room and rifled through his personal belongings.

In the suite, Walt located a few of the judge's unused EpiPens, his cell phone, and the discharge papers from his last visit to the emergency department. Before leaving, he gave Irena permission to ready the Windward Room for her next paying guest.

Glad that the judge's death wasn't going to cause her to lose money, Irena asked Paige and Alec, "Would you mind boxing up his things for his next of kin tomorrow? Afterward, I want Karine to give his room a thorough cleaning. God knows what he got up to in there!"

Paige hid her laugh and asked Aunt Irena, "Will you need either of us before teatime? Alec wants to speak to Joan about what it takes to be a beekeeper."

Irena warmed to the topic. Not suspecting a hidden motive on Alec's part, she declared, "Joan is so talented. She's a whiz at bookkeeping and was instrumental in designing my garden. We planted sunflowers, black eyed Susans, daisies, and zinnias—all the flowers that bees love. Joan's bees produce flavorful and healthy honey."

Irena stopped speaking for a moment and then added, "That is, healthy for everyone but Dick Cassidy."

On the way out of the inn, the DunBartons stopped to speak to Patrick. Though no one was expected to check in until Thursday afternoon, Patrick was busy searching the computer's internet. When Alec looked over his shoulder, he saw he was Googling— People who die in Maine without a will.

A huge amount of information populated the screen as Alec asked the young man, "What happened when Taylor interviewed you?"

With his face growing red from embarrassment, Patrick confided, "He told me that the police haven't been able to find a next of kin other than me. Officers went through the judge's Lincoln County Courthouse employment records and his personnel files while he was a district attorney in Cumberland County. The only thing my father ever signed of a personal nature was the lump sum child support agreement he filed in family court eighteen years ago.

"The police haven't exhausted all its avenues to find a will or closer living relative, but Walt thought I should familiarize myself with burial and cremation laws, just in case."

Overwhelmed, he resumed, "I'd rather be going over the lines in my play. The problems of Algernon Moncrieff were nothing compared to mine."

Alec and Paige commiserated with him and promised to help in any way they could. Hoping to talk to Patrick's mother next,

Alec excused themselves and took a winding and bee-lined path to the Bishop's house.

Her home was closer than Alec anticipated. Not more than twenty-five feet separated Joan's backyard from the Land's End property line. The sound of buzzing honey bees was almost deafening as the couple approached Joan's side door. Joan welcomed them into her kitchen and said, "Irena told me to expect you and that you wanted to learn all about bees. I can't wait to introduce you to my queen and her hive."

Alec became a bit alarmed when Joan asked, "Would you both like to suit up before I take you out to see them?"

Paige said she would happily watch from the kitchen window and Alec asked, "Can you tell us about them first? That way I'll be able to make sense of what you show me."

Joan agreed and invited the DunBartons to sit down at her small cheerful table. After serving them coffee and a plateful of store-bought cookies, Joan began, "Let's start with the easy stuff. Honey bees have a proboscis, which works like a tiny drinking straw and sucks up nectar from flowers. Bees have two stomachs. Some of the nectar goes in the bee's main stomach to digest it for food and energy. The rest goes into a special stomach where the bee can process the nectar into honey and transport it back to the hive."

Taking a cookie from the plate, Alec asked, "Do bees fly at night?"

"Oh, you mean last night," Joan resumed. "Bees can detect changes in the air. If it's going to rain or the temperature goes below 50 degrees, they like to stay in their hives. During the winter, they cluster together to stay warm, and nourish themselves with some of the honey they had produced earlier.

"That said, a bee will sting people and animals to protect themselves and their hive."

Paige murmured, "I see. I wonder if the judge swatted at one while we were watching the fireworks."

"I gave Walt Taylor a dead bee I found on the balcony deck," Alec admitted. "It looked a bit squashed."

Joan replied, "The stingers of honey bees are barbed and once they embed themselves in a person's skin, it becomes lodged. The bee not only loses its stinger when it tries to flee, but also its abdomen. Although the bee dies immediately, the stinger can continue to deliver venom."

Paige grimaced while Alec urged, "Tell us more. Is the queen bee more dangerous than her workers?"

Joan laughed, "Only if you're a drone bee. I see I need to give you a crash course on who does what in the hive."

As the DunBarton's coffee mugs were refilled, the twosome learned that a colony usually contains one queen bee, a few thousand drone bees or males, and tens of thousands of female worker bees. Joan went on to explain, "Worker bees carry on several functions within the hive. Depending on their age, they can feed the brood, receive nectar, clean the hive, act as a guard, and forage for food. The male or drone bee doesn't have a stinger and only exists to mate with the queen."

When Joan mentioned that drones died in the act of mating, Alec demanded to know more. He was astounded to hear that honey bee intercourse took place in mid-air. On a nuptial flight, the queen flies out in search of mates, and the drones swarm around her to compete for the chance to mate with her.

If a drone is successful, the force of the sex act causes his reproductive organ to be ripped from his body. The drone falls to the ground where it dies quickly, and the queen continues to mate with a dozen more drones. In that one night, a queen is able to collect enough sperm to fertilize all the eggs she will lay for the rest of her life.

Upon hearing all the details, Alec sang out,

She'll only come out at nights
The lean and hungry type
Nothing is new
I've seen her here before
Watching and waiting
Ooh, she's sittin' with you

But her eyes are on the door

So many have paid to see
What you think
You're getting' for free
The woman is wild
A she-cat tamed
By the purr of a Jaguar
Money's the matter
If you're in it for love
You ain't gonna get too far

(Oh-oh, here she comes)
Watch out boy
She'll chew you up
(Oh-oh, here she comes)
She's a maneater
(Oh-oh, here she comes)
Watch out boy
She'll chew you up
(Oh-oh, here she comes)
She's a maneater

I wouldn't if I were you
I know what she can do
She's deadly man
And she could really rip your world apart
Mind over matter
Ooh, the beauty is there
But a beast is in the heart

(Oh-oh, here she comes)
Watch out boy
She'll chew you up
(Oh-oh, here she comes)
She's a maneater
(Oh-oh, here she comes)
Watch out boy
She'll chew you up
(Oh-oh, here she comes)
She's a maneater

Slightly embarrassed, Paige apologized to Joan for her husband's outburst.

Joan was too busy laughing and then replied, "He's not wrong. In a bee colony, all sorts of behaviors can be observed. At least my bees are just driven by instinct and not malice, like some so-called human beings."

Certain she was referring to Dick Cassidy, Alec put on a white, heavy-duty, cotton-polyester suit to observe the bees up close. With the helmet and round veil on his head, Alec looked like he was an alien from a foreign world. Paige was happy to watch Joan and her brave husband from the safety of the kitchen.

When Alec returned, he was full of admiration for the tiny creatures. As he removed his outerwear, Alec graciously thanked Joan for her time and the information. Despite wanting to know how far Joan would go for Patrick to inherit his father's estate, Alec held his tongue. Afterall, Cassidy was murdered by a female worker bee, not a beekeeper.

The DunBartons returned to Land's End Inn just as afternoon tea was about to be served. Karine had helped Irena get the tea things together and plate the Almond Slices that Alec had made in the morning. The only guests present at tea was the young couple from Minnesota.

After asking them what they had done during the day, Alec discovered that they had visited the Coastal Maine Botanical Gardens. The morning's rain hadn't dampened their spirits and they felt a trip to the garden was well worth it.

Since Aunt Irena was not expecting new arrivals for another two days, she encouraged Alec and Paige to go out for dinner that evening and see the gardens the following day. Irena suggested several nice restaurants for them to try, and Alec and Paige headed to their suite to change for dinner.

Muddled about the many places that Irena had mentioned, Paige opened the bound Welcome Packet that was on the bed when they first arrived. While Alec was shaving in the bathroom, Paige called out, "There's lots of interesting information in this book about the inn and Boothbay Harbor in general. Even though it says that smoking is prohibited on the balconies, I'll ask Aunt Irena whether you can enjoy your pipe on our portion of the deck."

Alec emerged from the bathroom with shaving cream on both cheeks long enough to say, "I hope she won't mind. I've been longing to have a smoke with my whisky. In the meantime, did you find a good place to eat?"

Paige continued to thumb through the pages and when Alec returned with clean cheeks, she asked, "What are you in the mood for? There's Italian, Chinese, and a slew of seafood and lobster places."

Looking over his wife's shoulder at the restaurant listings, Alec said, "Let's try Robinson's Wharf. It's a working lobster pier with a full-service restaurant, pub, and gift store. And it's only ten minutes away by car."

Eager to have a traditional lobster dinner, Alec rushed Paige out of their suite and collected Irena's car keys. After bringing up Google maps in her vehicle and listening to the first set of directions, the twosome set off for a casual dinner.

The drive was interesting. Route 27 South twisted and turned before taking the DunBartons over a bridge to Southpoint Island. Alec had some trouble finding a parking spot near the popular eatery but was nevertheless thrilled by the restaurant's relaxed and scenic atmosphere.

Although the pier was surrounded by a thick mist, they were able to find a covered table that was protected from the elements. There were boats of every description bobbing in the sea and the place felt magical.

The DunBartons ordered steamed lobster dinners that included 1½ pound lobsters, fresh corn on the cob, and a side of coleslaw. While they waited for their meal, Paige had a Pratt's Island Punch, full of rum and tropical juices, and Alec his Scotch whisky.

Despite the cool temperatures, the couple dug into their meal with gusto. Alec had no trouble taking apart the crustacean with the nutcracker and a two-prong fork. He ate every part that was edible, along with the green tomalley in the lobster's cavity. Paige was less voracious, delicately removing the sweet lobster flesh from the claws and dunking each small piece in a plastic cup filled with melted butter.

After wiping her fingers on a number of paper napkins, Paige reached for her phone, looked up tomalley, and read to Alec, "You're eating the equivalent of a lobster's liver and pancreas. If it's tainted by PSP, paralytic shellfish poison, it can make you dizzy and nauseous."

Undaunted, Alec swallowed the last bit of tomalley and responded, "Single-malt scotch kills all germs, Lass."

Paige merely sighed, used to Alec's untrue statements about his native drink. When all that remained of Alec's meal were the shells, Paige handed her husband a disposable hand wipe, and asked, "Are you going to have dessert?"

Alec glanced at the menu for a moment and replied, "The choices look interesting, but I think I'll have leftover Almond Slices when we return to the inn. They're not too sweet and go well with Glenlivet.

The pair sat in companionable silence on the way back to the Land's End Bed and Breakfast until Alec spotted a sign for St. Andrew's Urgent Care Center where the judge was first treated for anaphylaxis. Still unable to shake the feeling that Richard Cassidy's death was orchestrated by someone who attended the July fourth festivities, Alec pronounced, "There may be a killer among us."

Paige shivered in response.

CHAPTER SEVEN

▼

"These Eyes"
Words & Music by Randy Bachman & Burton Cummings
Genre: Rock, Released: December 1968

Wednesday Afternoon—6th of July

The morning passed by quickly. After making Ham and Cheese Parcels, Blueberry Pancakes, and Pumpkin Cranberry Loaves for the inn's patrons, Alec sought out Paige and found her with Karine "fluffing up" Room 5.

Paige had just checked off the column's box: "Raise blinds, lock windows, and exit," when Alec appeared.

Rooms Requiring Cleaning								
New Arrival: Flip Current Guest: Fluff			Room 1	Room 2	Room 3	Room 4	Room 5	Room 6
Fluff:								
	Return TV remote to cabinet						X	
	Empty trash cans, Replace glassware						X	
	Make bed						X	
	Vacuum carpet and mop bathroom floor						X	
	Clean toilet, sink, and counter						X	
	Replace soaps, shampoo, toilet paper and tissues						X	
	Replace makeup removers, sanitary boxes, etc.						X	
	Replace used towels						X	
	Raise blinds, lock windows, and exit						X	

Rooms Requiring Cleaning							
New Arrival: Flip **Current Guest: Fluff**		Room 1	Room 2	Room 3	Room 4	Room 5	Room 6
Flip: Fluff and add							
	Check under bed for dust and lost items						
	Change bed linens/make bed						
	Dust all furniture, window sills, ceiling fan						
	Disinfect bathtub, shower walls, and rails						
	Disinfect toilet, sink counter, and mirror						
	Change bathtub rug, if needed						
	Replace bathrobes						
	Mop bathroom floor						
	Place pen by the guest book						
	Adjust thermostat						
	Check lights work						
	Make sure alarm clocks are not set to go off						
	Hang pictures straight						

After gazing at Paige's cheat sheet, Alec asked, "What's the difference between 'Fluff' and 'Flip, Fluff, and Add?'"

Karine answered for Paige and explained, "Fluff is for visitors who are staying another night or a few more days. I do a thorough cleaning when a guest checks out and a new one is expected to arrive."

Alec nodded and watched Karine drop Hillary's used towels in the laundry chute before asking, "Would you mind if I borrow Paige? Irena wants us to pack up the judge's belongings before we visit the botanical gardens."

Karine, smiled, "Better you than me. The judge ordered me to stay out of his suite and to leave fresh towels outside his door every other day. When you finish in there, I plan to fumigate the room."

Not sure what the judge may have done to the housekeeper, Alec decided to question her later and induced his wife to enter the Windward Room where Cassidy had been staying. The suite was exceptionally clean. Alec found two of the judge's empty suitcases in the closet and proceeded to place one of them on the unmade bed to pack it.

As Paige handed Alec the judge's perfectly folded shirts and sweaters from a chest of drawers, she murmured, "He was very tidy, and the labels indicate he spared no expense to have the best quality."

Alec agreed. "I wonder if we'll find out anything new about the man from his clothes."

Upon emptying the closet, the twosome entered the bathroom, where two empty vodka bottles were dumped in the trash can. Alec gathered up Cassidy's toiletries, shaver, and hairbrush, wondering whether Richard could have been poisoned over a long period of time.

Remembering that the OCME was going to run toxicology tests, Alec dropped the thought. Annoyed to have found nothing of interest in the bathroom, Alec then examined his refrigerator. It was full of nearly empty mixers and packages of half-eaten cheese.

After placing them in the trash, Alec opened the drawers of the end tables, and stripped the bed. Caught between the comforter and sheets, at the foot of the bed, was an interior design magazine.

Alec flipped through the worn pages and was astounded to see an article on Hillary Fairchild. On each page, where her photo appeared, her face was scratched out with a black marker. On the last page he wrote, "Bitch, you'll pay!"

At one o'clock, Alec and Paige headed over to the Coastal Maine Botanical Gardens. On the way to the tourist sight, the DunBartons discussed what they had found in Cassidy's room.

It was obvious from the vehemence in which the decorator's face was marred that the judge was a deeply disturbed man. Alec had left word at the police station for Walt to contact him and wondered whether Hillary had feared for her life.

Those thoughts turned to happier ones when the DunBartons made a left onto Botanical Gardens Drive and parked near the visitor center. After purchasing their tickets and receiving a map of the grounds, Alec and Paige crossed over an arced wooden bridge to get to the beautiful, manicured gardens.

The colors and fragrances of the flowers were amazing. The bees must have thought so too. Each side of the pathway was filled with buzzing insects intent on filling their proboscises with nectar.

Walking in single file to keep away from the honeybees, Alec commented, "I doubt this place was ever a favorite haunt of the Honorable Richard Cassidy."

Paige agreed and stopped to photograph the pond in the Garden of the Five Senses, "It's lovely here but not for those allergic to insect venom. I think a mosquito just bit me!"

Alec dove into Paige's well-packed tote bag and happily pulled out a bottle of bug spray. As he handed it to his wife, he whispered in her ear, "I'm the only one allowed to nibble on you."

The couple made a point of visiting each of the huge wooden trolls that inhabited the grounds while also acquainting themselves with the butterfly house, bee exhibit, and fairy village. After meandering along the grounds for almost two hours, Alec pleaded, "It's quite muggy here despite the cool temperature. Let's get something to drink at the café."

Hearing no argument from his wife, Alec directed Paige to the eatery. Even though it wasn't a particularly inviting restaurant, they were able to get cold beverages and take seats outside the cramped building where they could admire the scenery.

With renewed vigor, the DunBartons decided to hike along one of the woodland trails. It was 4:05 PM when they returned to the car and Alec worried aloud, "I hope your aunt is able to serve afternoon tea without us. I hate to disappoint the 'old girl.'"

Paige laughed, "Don't let her hear you say that. I saw pictures of Irena when she was in her twenties. She was breathtaking. Irena loved only one man in her life. She met James, her beau, in college and they later quit school to work on a commune. They grew up in the hippie era.

"My aunt was so happy when they became engaged. It didn't last long though. In 1969, the government instituted the draft lottery. Her fiancée's number was very low, and he was drafted. It broke my aunt's heart when James was killed in action. She never loved anyone else."

Alec had not known about her sad past. Thinking about the loss she must have endured when James didn't return, Alec recalled a sixties song about loss and sang,

These eyes cry every night for you
These arms long to hold you again
The hurtin's on me, yeah
But I will never be free, no, my baby, no, no
You gave a promise to me, yeah
And you broke it, you broke it, oh, no

These eyes watched you bring my world to an end
This heart could not accept and pretend
The hurtin's on me, yeah
But I will never be free, no, no, no
You took the vow with me, yeah
And you spoke it, you spoke it, babe

These eyes are cryin'
These eyes have seen a lot of loves
But they're never gonna see another one like I had with you

Upon returning to the inn, Alec greeted Paige's aunt with a warm hug. With a shy smile, Irena whispered to Paige, "We should let him out of the house more often."

Though the DunBartons were late for teatime, Irena was able to put out the refreshments with Patrick's help. The last few pieces of the defrosted Sour Cream Coffee Cake were on the sideboard along with a pot of hot water, the creamers, and sugar.

Alec tasted a slice of the cake and pronounced it delicious. The Pierces excused themselves after finishing their tea and the young couple departed a few minutes later, eager to enjoy their last night in Boothbay Harbor.

When Alec asked about Hillary Fairchild, Irena giggled. "She left a few minutes ago to meet Police Chief Taylor for an early dinner at an Italian restaurant in the center of town."

Now ready to hear some gossip, Alec took a seat close to Irena's wheelchair and asked, "Is Walt single? I want to hear all about him."

While Paige refilled Alec's teacup, Irena answered, "Walt Taylor grew up in Queens, New York, and was a detective at the NYC Police Department. When his wife sued him for divorce, he decided to change his life and relocate to Maine, where his grandparents had a summer home. As a boy, he used to visit them during school vacations. He was a cute, well-behaved boy."

Sighing, Irena recalled, "It seems like only yesterday, he was a young man. Now, his only daughter is a beautiful woman. She just finished college in Colorado and plans to teach elementary school there."

To himself, Alec muttered, "I wonder whether Walt is going to fall for Hillary. If she found a way to murder Cassidy and make it appear to be an accident, it will be hard to prove, especially if she has bewitched the police chief."

Alec and Paige put all thoughts of murder and mayhem away while they purchased items on Irena's grocery list. They found Hannaford's Market a pleasant place to shop. In the wine and liquor aisle, Alec checked the price of the store's Glenlivet and was pleased to see it was one dollar less than those he had purchased in town. Unable to pass up even the smallest deal, he bought two more for himself and a bottle of gin for Paige.

After putting away the groceries in the inn's kitchen, Alec placed two hot rotisserie chickens on a table in the breakfast room along with two one-pound sides of potato salad and coleslaw. When the table was set, Paige summoned Patrick and Irena over to eat.

Dinner was a jolly affair even though the topic of conversation was a bit creepy. Patrick was talkative, full of information about who can obtain a death certificate in Maine and how to get multiple copies for the banks.

While pulling the chicken leg from its thigh, Patrick regaled, "I would have been allowed to order copies of the death certificate as a direct descendent, but I'm too young. You have to be twenty-five years old. I think my mother is going to speak to a lawyer on my behalf. So far the police haven't discovered any other living relatives for my father."

When Patrick referred to the judge as "my father," Alec began to see Richard Cassidy as more than a flawed individual. He must have had friends or someone who cared about him. Eager to speak to Walt Taylor, Alec asked Patrick, "Has the Office of the Chief Medical Examiner in Augusta concluded their report? They can't issue a death certificate till then."

Patrick agreed. "Walt said they should have the final results tomorrow. The judge had a high level of trip…tase or something like that in his blood. Whatever it was, it's usually in the tox screens of people who were stung by bees."

Certain that Cassidy wasn't poisoned by another substance, Alec concluded, "It looks like your father's death was purely accidental."

Irena responded vehemently, "Of course, it was an accident! You can't make a bee sting anyone on purpose."

The intensity of her statement caused Alec to wonder whether Aunt Irena knew something he didn't.

When everyone had their fill of chicken, Paige and Alec cleared the table and put away the leftovers. To get a start on the following day's menu, the DunBartons made the peach filling for the turnovers and prepared the hash brown crust for the cheddar cheese quiche. They had just turned off the kitchen lights and were near the foyer when Walt Taylor and Hillary Fairchild entered the inn.

Hillary, appearing a bit startled at seeing them, quickly thanked the police chief for dinner and scampered up the steps to the second-floor landing. Wisely, Paige excused herself to look in on her aunt, leaving Alec alone with Taylor.

Before Walt could turn and go, Alec suggested, "Would you care to join me for a drink? I have something to show you and would like to know how your investigation is proceeding."

Glad the police chief was receptive, Alec directed him to his suite's third-floor balcony.

CHAPTER EIGHT

▼

"The End of Innocence"
Words & Music by Don Henley and Bruce Hornby
Genre: Rock, Released: June 1989

__Wednesday Evening—6th of July__

When Alec and Walt were comfortably ensconced on the balcony outside the DunBarton's suite with drinks, Alec asked, Would you mind if I smoked?"

Walt shook his head, "As long as you're not breaking the inn's smoking policy. I would hate to run you in for that."

Alec, uncertain whether the police chief was being serious, laughed uneasily and remarked, "Paige's aunt just gave me permission to smoke in this section of the deck."

Once his pipe was stuffed with his favorite cherry tobacco, Alec lit it with two matches and showed Walt the interior decorating magazine he had found in the judge's room. Walt did not appear surprised by how violently Hillary's face had been disfigured on the magazine's pages.

The chief took a long draught from his scotch and replied, "As you may have suspected, I'm off duty now and your detective friend in Fort Lauderdale said I can confide in you. With that said,

I'd like to share with you just how loathsome Richard Cassidy was."

Alec sat up attentively and learned that a number of complaints had been lodged against Judge Cassidy. Some people had accused him of improper behavior in the courtroom—drunk on the bench and rude and abusive to attorneys and their clients. Off the bench, he had used his position to threaten others, influence judicial decisions, obstruct justice, and exhort favors.

Walt's eyes turned steely when he added, "Cassidy tried to coerce me to look the other way when several women in town complained of unwanted attention from him. As you may know, I also had words with him when Miss Fairchild was being cyberstalked. One woman in the neighboring town claimed he had raped her. She later withdrew her charge, and I was unable to do anything about it.

"Over the last few years, the Maine Supreme Judicial Court has reviewed some of the judicial misconduct complaints that were levied against Cassidy. Up until now, he had only been given a slap on the wrist. A few of them were still pending when Cassidy met his untimely death. If he had been murdered, I would have looked at his many victims first."

Alec mulled over his statement and then asked, "Did Irena's guests and neighbors have a more personal interest to want the judge dead?"

Stretching his long legs in front of him, Walt confided, "Most of them had reason to loathe him. Karine's husband, a lobsterman, had a run-in with Cassidy over his business practices, Joan Bishop was unable to get more child support from him, and Patrick was aware that his father felt he was a 'loser.' On top of that, the judge was in the process of suing Chip Granger."

Alec, noting that he had failed to mention Irena Anderson, the Pierces, and Hillary Fairchild, remarked, "There may have been others who hated the judge. I just can't figure out how a killer could have made his death appear to be an accident. Did the EpiPens contain the proper amount of epinephrine?"

Walt replied, "The OCME lab checked its contents. The pens had not been tampered with. The dead bee you found was missing its stinger, indicating it had made contact with the judge's skin. The corpse was examined thoroughly, and the entry point was swollen, yet visible. The lab took samples of Cassidy's blood and found it contained high levels of tryptase, an enzyme that's released when it comes into contact with an allergen.

"That, along with the witness statements and his medical history has been enough to convince the medical examiner to complete the death certificate tomorrow and release the body without conducting an autopsy. Since the judge did not have a will and no other heirs have popped up, Patrick Bishop has been given the go ahead to become the executor of Cassidy's rather large estate."

Alec relit his pipe and blew a smoke ring to digest the information. It looked like the young man was going to have enough money to pay for acting college. It also left Alec to wonder whether Joan Bishop was going to use some of her son's windfall to buy Irena's bed and breakfast.

Since Walt didn't have anything to say about his recent "date" with Hillary, Alec questioned, "I don't suppose you have a high crime rate in Boothbay Harbor."

Walt seemed to relax as their conversation shifted to the general topic of law enforcement and had Alec top off his drink. While Alec refilled his own, Walt confirmed, "We have our share of thefts and assaults, but murders are very rare. The last one occurred when a troubled resident killed his wife and son before committing suicide. He didn't want to face the consequences of his actions and took the 'easy' way out.

"The low crime rate is what attracted me here in the first place," Walt continued. "I graduated from John Jay College of Criminal Justice in New York and worked my way up in the NYC Police Department. The amount of crime in the city was staggering, and I wasn't the easiest man to live with. When I wrecked my marriage, I decided to move up here permanently. My grandparents left me a small place in Boothbay."

Alec shared some of his personal history as well and let Walt know that he had only been married to Paige a year and a half. Upon telling him that his previous wife and young daughter were killed by a drunk driver in London, the police chief sympathized and acknowledged that his college-aged daughter was instrumental in helping him rebuild his life.

The men sat in companionable silence until Paige returned to their suite to remind Alec that he had to make breakfast in the morning. Before going their separate ways, Alec asked Walt to keep him posted if new information came to light.

After combining the ingredients for the cheddar cheese and bacon quiche in a bowl, Alec poured the mixture onto the prepared crust and popped it in the preheated oven. The time was 8:00 AM.

Paige was equally busy in the kitchen. Under Irena's guidance, she had prepared the Cinnamon Crescent Rolls. With her fingers encrusted in melted butter, cinnamon, and chopped pecans, Paige declared, "Running a B&B is not easy."

Turning to her aunt, Paige questioned, "How did you manage to do this all by yourself."

Irena smiled sweetly and answered, "It gets easier, dear. You and Alec have only been at it for four days."

To Alec, it seemed a lot longer. Having a few minutes to rest, Alec poured himself a cup of hot coffee. Not sure it was a good time to bring it up, Alec related to Irena, "I had an interesting conversation with Officer Taylor last night, It looks like the OCME is going to release the judge's body today. Patrick will have to dispose of his corpse and apply to become executor of his estate. He'll have to grow up fast."

Irena sighed, "The poor boy. I'm afraid, he's going to lose his innocence."

That's all Alec had to hear before belting out,

Remember when the days were long
And rolled beneath a deep blue sky
Didn't have a care in the world

With mommy and daddy standin' by
But "happily ever after" fails
And we've been poisoned by these fairy tales
The lawyers dwell on small details
Since daddy had to fly

But I know a place where we can go
That's still untouched by men
We'll sit and watch the clouds roll by
And the tall grass waves in the wind
You can lay your head back on the ground
And let your hair fall all around me
Offer up your best defense
But this is the end
This is the end of the innocence

O' beautiful, for spacious skies
But now those skies are threatening
They're beating plowshares into swords
For this tired old man that we elected king
Armchair warriors often fail
And we've been poisoned by these fairy tales
The lawyers clean up all details
Since daddy had to lie

But I know a place where we can go
And wash away this sin
We'll sit and watch the clouds roll by
And the tall grass waves in the wind
Just lay your head back on the ground
And let your hair spill all around me
Offer up your best defense
But this is the end
This is the end of the innocence

Who knows how long this will last
Now we've come so far, so fast
But, somewhere back there in the dust
That same small town in each of us
I need to remember this
So baby give me just one kiss
And let me take a long last look
Before we say goodbye

Just lay your head back on the ground
And let your hair fall all around me
Offer up your best defense
But this is the end
This is the end of the innocence

Alec finished the last verse at the same time that the kitchen timer buzzed. Paige's first batch of cinnamon rolls were ready to come out of the oven. While placing the pan on a wire rack to cool, Alec swiped one from the tray to have with his coffee. Paige shook her head as Alec polished it off and warned, "We might not have enough for the guests."

Irena stood up for Alec and intervened, "Nonsense! We can always make more."

Their banter was interrupted when Patrick entered the kitchen earlier than usual. He looked tired and the sparkle in his eyes was not quite as bright.

Since none of the B&B occupants were up yet and demanding attention, Alec asked the lad what was causing his distress. It didn't take long for him to enumerate his concerns.

Chief among them was how and where to dispose of his father's body. He was reluctant to do what his mother proposed. She felt it fitting to cremate Cassidy and have his ashes scattered in their flower bed, where the bees could finish off what they had started.

Alec nearly laughed but was able to hold in his mirth. Although it would cost the Bishops more, Alec suggested a quick and inexpensive burial. Cremations were so final, and Alec still had concerns about the way Cassidy had died. If necessary, a corpse could always be exhumed and autopsied later.

Young Bishop appeared even more miserable as he took his place at the front desk and opened the inn's computer.

First to arrive for breakfast were the Pierces. They both had the Cheddar Cheese and Bacon Quiche and didn't dawdle over their meal since they planned to take a day trip to Camden, a scenic town on Penobscot Bay, north of Boothbay Harbor. They didn't expect to be back until late and told Irena that they would miss teatime.

Hillary, anxious to pick up something she ordered from a shop in Wiscasset, asked Paige if she wanted to join her. Eager to have female companionship. Paige accepted right away. They departed after Paige placed the last dirty dish in the dishwasher.

As Irena was seeing off the young couple from St. Paul, Minnesota, Alec learned from Patrick that a middle-aged couple from California was going to be staying in the judge's newly vacant room, and a chatty woman by the name of Nancy was going to occupy Portside Retreat. Patrick was glad that Irena had changed the minimum stay for the summer season from one to two nights. One-nighters caused more work, and he already had too much on his plate.

When Alec finished his morning chores, he walked over to the first-floor balcony to relax in a padded chair. As he was watching the tide in the inner harbor recede, he heard the buzz of a grass edger coming from Joan's property.

Curious, Alec took the outdoor staircase to the second-floor landing and gazed over the fence to see Chip Granger tidying up her yard. He looked almost comical. Chip had to fully extend the edger from his body to both trim the path and stay away from the bees.

Upon hearing Alec's call, Chip turned off the machine. The handyman seemed happy to see him and invited, "Hey, let's go out for lunch and a drink when I finish here. This work makes me powerfully thirsty."

Alec agreed and told him to come by as soon as he was done. About thirty minutes later, Chip showed up at the inn, sunburned and a bit sweaty. After chatting a few minutes about where to go for lunch, the two men headed over to Footbridge Brewery.

Alec and Chip found a table outside the brewery that was shaded from the sun. When their sixteen-ounce beers arrived, Chip took a long draught and wiped the foam from his upper lip with the back of his hand. Still thirsty, he drank some more and said, "What's happening with Judge Cassidy's estate? Is the kid going to inherit?"

Alec was surprised he knew so much until he realized that word of mouth probably travelled fast in the small town of Boothbay Harbor. Chip's beer was almost gone by the time their sandwich wraps arrived. After asking for another beer from a female server, he obviously knew well, the two men sampled their wraps. Alec had a chicken curry wrap and Chip, one with tuna.

While enjoying their meals, Alec turned Chip's attention away from Patrick and said to the handyman, "You must be relieved that Cassidy can't sue you from the grave."

Chip found Alec's statement humorous and nearly choked on a potato chip. When he was able to respond, he launched into a five-minute rant, calling the judge every name in the book while painting himself as totally innocent.

When he calmed down, Alec discovered that Chip was being sued one hundred thousand dollars for sloppy plumbing work, which caused a leak and the eventual growth of black mold in the lower level of Cassidy's house.

Angrily, Chip related, "The cleanup was only supposed to take two weeks and cost twenty thousand dollars. He turned a little accident into a federal case. He asked the remediation team to do more than what was required. Dick not only sued me for damages but also pain and suffering."

Over his third beer, Chip intimated, 'The judge used the mold incident to book a room at Land's End Inn where he could spy on his estranged son and his ex-lady friend. That man thought he could do anything he wanted to anyone he pleased."

Even though Alec ended up paying for the two meals, he felt the cost was well worth it.

When Alec returned to the inn, he found his wife having a cozy tête-à-tête with Hillary in the breakfast room. The two were having tea and leftover Sour Cream Coffee Cake from the day before. Alec didn't want to disturb them but also wanted to know how far the judge had gone to make the interior decorator's life miserable. Hillary Fairchild was no shrinking violet. From what Alec had observed, she was the kind of woman who knew what she wanted.

Alec listened near the door while Patrick eyed him from the front desk. Upon hearing that their conversation was simply about the beauties of Maine, Alec stepped into the room with a sweet smile and asked, "Can I join you ladies?"

Paige motioned to the chair beside her in response and said, "I know teatime is in two hours, but we couldn't wait. Would you like something?"

Since Alec wasn't particularly hungry, he took a small slice of cake. Hillary gazed at Alec as if seeing him for the first time and smiled wickedly. "Paige has told me a lot about you. You're some sort of sleuth and work on a cruise ship?"

Alec nodded while Hillary continued. "Cassidy's death must be driving you crazy! If he was murdered, it was a perfect one—dressed up to look like an accident.

"I understand what it feels like to deceive others," Hillary resumed. "As an interior decorator, I often fool the eyes of my clients by making small spaces appear larger. At other times, I have my contractors knock down walls, which dramatically change how a home functions. If Cassidy was murdered, I can't imagine how you're going to prove it."

Alec took on a new appreciation for what Hillary did for a living and asked how she became an interior decorator. She revealed what it was like to grow up in London and then move to New York when she married a famous attorney.

Despite being successful and having a home decorating retail store in the city, Hillary remarked, "It's not enough. I'm tired of traveling from place to place for my business and when I return to my apartment in NYC, it feels empty."

Paige agreed. "As a cruise consultant on the Pegasus, I was often lonely. The ship changed itineraries twice a year, but every day was like the day before it. People came and went. It was not until I met Alec that I truly felt at home. It didn't matter where we were. Home was where my heart was."

Hillary sighed, "I hope it's not too late for me."

Alec took her last statement as an invitation to ask, "Did you ever think that Richard Cassidy might figure in your future?"

Wrinkling her nose in disgust, "Hillary replied, "Not for a minute. I only accepted his original offer to dinner in hopes of finding more clients. When we went out, he liked to show me off and introduce me to his associates. I can't deny he was charming at first. He knew exactly what buttons to push to ingratiate himself.

"After I told Dick I wasn't interested in having a relationship, he continued to bother me in New York. At the beginning, he just phoned and texted. When he followed up with flowers and chocolate, I warned him again. I became more alarmed when he learned which homes I was redecorating and who I was seeing. I think he somehow got hold of my phone records. When he told one of my male clients to fire me, I contacted the Boothbay Harbor Police."

Alec, uncertain as to why Hillary hadn't informed the judge's employers, inquired, "Why didn't you take it any further?"

"I would have," Hillary replied, "but I wanted to give the Boothbay Harbor police a chance first. Dick bragged that he knew everyone of importance, and I wasn't sure it would do any good."

Hillary confirmed, "It worked fine until I found out that Cassidy was staying at the inn. I had hoped to avoid him when I changed my standard reservation from September to July."

Anxiously, Paige queried, "What did you do when you saw him?"

Now smiling, Hillary recalled, "I told him to keep away from me and, if he didn't, I was going to press charges against him for cyberstalking. Somehow, he seemed less frightening in person, and I knew Irena had my back."

Paige agreed. "My aunt may look fragile, but she has always given me the strength to do what's necessary."

Eager to learn what Hillary thought of Irena's staff and the other guests at the inn, Alec posed the question. With clarity, the decorator remarked, "Patrick is a darling. He inherited his father's charm but none of his viciousness. Joan is a mystery to me and a bit quirky. I suppose she could have been taken in by Cassidy when she was young and foolish. I can't help wondering if she placed a dead bee on the judge's chair. Could a stinger from the insect still inflict damage?"

Alec had considered that same thing but thought it unlikely. The judge had been standing when he cried out in pain, and he didn't think a stinger from a dead bee was rigid enough to puncture a pair of trousers.

Hillary resumed, "I suppose, anyone on the balcony could have done it. Even me. As to Karine, the housekeeper, she hated the judge. I heard them have it out in the second-floor parlor earlier that afternoon."

When questioned about what they had been talking about, Hillary shrugged. "I just heard the word *blackmail*."

Paige shuddered. "He was certainly a disagreeable person. Do you know anything about Chip Granger? He's sort of a clown and loves being the center of attention."

"He's more than that," Hillary warned. "He comes across as harmless, but he's a womanizer. I heard he had affairs with several of the women in town. I think Joan welcomed his advances the last time I was here."

Aware that afternoon tea needed to be prepared shortly, Alec hurriedly stated, "That leaves the Pierces. What do you make of them?"

Closing her eyes in thought, the decorator replied, "Leanne is bright even though she appears scatterbrained. She could be a very successful business woman if she wasn't so invested in her husband and children. The doctor, however, is another story. He always seems calm but under that quiet exterior, I think he's a man with strong desires."

Alec thanked Hillary Fairchild for her insights. She had given him a lot to think about.

CHAPTER NINE

▼

"Easy To Be Hard"
Words & Music by James Rado,
Gerome Ragni, and Galt MacDermot
Genre: Rock, Released: August 1969

Friday Morning—8th of July

Alec woke up feeling annoyed. There were two possibilities. Either Cassidy met his maker by accident and Alec was wasting his time or someone murdered the judge, and it was going to be impossible to prove. Nevertheless, Alec needed to talk to Karine, the housekeeper, to find out why she had argued with Judge Cassidy on the afternoon of his death.

While preparing the Broccoli Frittata and Peach Waffles with Irena's help, Alec gazed out the kitchen window watching for Karine Rybakov to approach the inn. The Russian woman was not a person to be trifled with. She was fiercely loyal to her husband, family, and friends. Although Irena was her employer, Karine counted Paige's aunt among her closest friends.

Luckily for Alec, Karine came in fifteen minutes early and Paige was able to take over Alec's kitchen duties for a short while. The housekeeper helped herself to coffee and some newly baked Irish Soda Bread and butter. Alec joined her at an outside table by the first-floor parlor. None of the guests were up yet and Alec was not going to let the opportunity slip by.

Karine must have picked up on Alec's doggedness and asked, "Have I done something wrong?"

Alec smiled, hoping to reduce the tension, and replied, "Not at all. I was just wondering what you and Cassidy argued about on the day of his death."

The housekeeper's ruddy cheeks turned a darker red as she made a move to stand up. After a moment, Karine then settled back in her seat and voiced, "I owe a lot to Irena and I'm only going to answer your question because she has high regard for you. If you upset her, you'll have to deal with me. Do you understand?"

Alec was taken aback by her words and realized that the judge had threatened Paige's aunt and not Karine. Worried for the first time that Irena had knowingly given Cassidy raw honey in her spice cake, Alec demanded, "What did the judge have on Irena?"

Slowly, Karine explained, "It wasn't just one thing. First, he accused Irena of price fixing. Over the winter, your aunt met with some friends in town who run B&Bs. They only determined that rooms with whirlpool tubs and sitting areas were worth more than rooms that didn't have extra amenities.

"I don't know how he found out, but he said she had participated in price fixing and had violated the federal Sherman Anti-Trust Law. Irena was on her stepladder, reaching for a platter, when he had threatened her. She was so rattled by him; she fell off the stool and broke her ankle.

Alec found himself getting angrier and angrier as Karine continued, "The judge also told her she was incompliant with the Americans with Disabilities Act (ADA) by not having a ramp at the front entrance. That turned out to be hogwash. As you know, we have one guest room that's on the ground level and handicapped guests can enter the inn from the kitchen door ramp. He just wanted to get a rise from your poor aunt."

Recalling that Hillary had overheard the word blackmail during the argument, Alec asked, "Did the judge try to extort money from Irena?"

Karine appeared confused by the question and then responded, "Oh, that happened later when Cassidy said he saw my husband cut another man's lobster line and wanted money to keep his mouth shut. I laughed when he accused Ivan. I knew the judge was full of it and told him so."

Aware that the inn's guests were stirring, Alec thanked the housekeeper for her frankness and headed back to the kitchen. On the way, the lyrics to the Three Dog Night song came to mind and he sang,

How can people be so heartless
How can people be so cruel
Easy to be hard
Easy to be cold

How can people have no feelings
How can they ignore their friends
Easy to be proud
Easy to say no

Especially people who care about strangers
Who care about evil and social injustice
Do you only care about the bleeding crowd
How about a needy friend
I need a friend

How can people be so heartless
You know I'm hung up on you
Easy to be proud
Easy to say no

Especially people who care about strangers
Who care about evil and social injustice
Do you only care about the bleeding crowd
How about a needy friend
We all need a friend

How can people be so heartless
How can people be so cruel
Easy to be proud

> Easy to say no
> Easy to be cold
> Easy to say no
> Come on, easy to be mean
> Easy to say no
> Easy to be cold
> Easy to say no
> Much too easy to say no

Paige heard her husband crooning as he approached and said, "I'm glad you're back and can take over. I have to serve now."

Alec smiled at his wife who had flour on her nose and cheeks. After wiping them off, she slipped into the breakfast room to take down the meal orders, leaving Alec alone with Irena.

Irena gazed shyly at Alec and pronounced, "I had nothing to do with Cassidy's death. He was a mean, horrible man, and I'm glad that bee finished him off. I just hope that one of my guests or neighbors didn't orchestrate it."

Alec had to agree as he and Aunt Irena finished their cooking and baking chores for the day.

After cleaning the stainless-steel prep island and starting the dishwasher, Alec posed to Paige, "Let's do something fun this afternoon. Uncertain as to where to go, the couple perused the brochures in the inn's foyer. As they were looking at a few colorful flyers advertising places of interest, Patrick recommended, "You must visit the Railroad Museum and take a few boat excursions while you're here."

Since the weather was iffy and the following day promised to be sunny, Alec opened up the Railroad Village Museum pamphlet and glanced at the inside map. Surprised to see multiple buildings on the site and not just one stuffy museum, Alec turned to Patrick and asked, "Is it a restoration village?"

Patrick paused to answer a phone call and then replied, "There are about forty buildings on the property along with a working railroad train and a few animals. If you like old cars, there's also a huge barn full of stuff from the 1920's on."

Though Paige would have preferred to go on a boat ride, she agreed it would be better to go the following day. Alec waited for her in the foyer while she hurried up to their suite to collect essential items for their day trip.

Patrick went on to say, "The town of Boothbay Harbor uses the museum's village green for many of its events. Next weekend, the grounds are going to be the site of a book fair showcasing Maine authors. And in the autumn, the Vintage Market, Family Harvest Day, and Fall Foliage Festival are going to be held there. The Fall Festival is a lot of fun with homemade crafts, pumpkin carving, and great food."

Paige arrived as Patrick was finishing his sentence and sighed, "I would love to come back in the autumn when the leaves are falling, and you can feel the nip in the air."

Suddenly visualizing his seductive wife by a roaring wood fireplace, "Alec kissed the top of Paige's head and hoarsely said, "Let's get going and have a late lunch somewhere."

The couple found the Railway Village Museum easily. Paige recalled seeing it when she and Hillary had passed it on their way to Wiscasset and had not realized how large the place was from the road. After parking, Alec and Paige entered the Freeport Train Depot to buy tickets and collect a sticker allowing them to visit the various buildings.

As the receptionist was returning Alec's credit card, a loud whistle from the incoming train announced it was about to stop in front of the depot. The woman behind the counter shook her head in distaste and placed her hands over her ears to decrease the noise, apparently annoyed every time the train pulled up.

Even though Alec wanted to hop onto the train right away, Paige held him back upon noticing Dr. Pierce and Leanne emerge from their car in the parking lot. Alec cheerfully greeted the couple when they came into the ticket office.

While Leanne paid for their tickets, Alan Pierce invited Alec and Paige to see the museum grounds with them. Alec was surprised to see the doctor so animated. When Leanne joined them, he added, "We always make a point to visit here on our yearly excursion to Boothbay Harbor. There are always new things to see."

Since the train only operated every hour on the hour, both couples mounted the waiting train. The loud whistle blew again as it left the station. Alan explained that it was going to make two rotations around its vast grounds. When the train made a sharp turn. Paige laughed and held onto Alec. The Pierces were full of information and pointed out places of interest along the way.

After completing the second and final trip, everyone got off and walked across the grassy lawn of the village green. Paige enjoyed their visit to the Harrington Homestead and Barn the most. The Maine farmhouse had been moved from across the street and contained furnishings and appliances from an earlier and simpler period. It was easy for the DunBartons to imagine what life was like during that time.

Alec found the school house, fire station, and Dingley's General Store fascinating. When the foursome mounted the hill by the Thorndike Train Station, both women decided to rest under a shade tree while the men strolled around the antique auto museum.

In the auto museum, Alec showed Alan a 1917 Ford Model T Touring Car that originally cost $350 and a 1931 New Ford, 4-Cylinder auto that had been listed for $450. A page from an old newspaper was mounted beside the 1931 car. Its headline was about the Ford Motor Company, but Alec found an article about Mussolini far more riveting.

Twenty minutes later, Alec and Alan collected their wives and continued on to the model railroad museum, where they watched toy trains chug past miniature houses, trees, and people. The trip back to the museum's entrance was pretty exhausting, The sun was out, and Leanne had to hold onto her husband's arm several times while walking along the uneven path.

Hungry and tired, Alec suggested lunch. Both Alan and Leanne readily agreed, and the two couples made arrangement to meet at Brady's, a restaurant that was walking distance from the Land's End Inn.

At two o'clock, the DunBartons welcomed Alan and Leanne to the outside table they were able to procure minutes earlier. They had a perfect view of the inner harbor and were shaded from the sun by a well-placed umbrella.

Although the lunch menu was limited, they had no trouble finding something to eat. While waiting for their entrees, everyone whetted their appetites with cold beer and fruity alcoholic beverages. Alec couldn't get over the change in the doctor. Now seated at the eatery, he was full of life and no longer tired or controlled.

Wondering whether Cassidy's behavior had caused the doctor to withdraw, Alec asked him if the judge's presence had affected him. Alan answered sincerely, "That man was a blight upon your aunt's bed and breakfast. He sucked all the air from the room. Irena and the housekeeper had to tiptoe around the judge."

Leanne confirmed her husband's sentiments and added, "When Hillary learned that Cassidy was staying at the inn, she turned white. She tried to book accommodations at a few other places only to learn that no one had vacancies. Irena apologized, but it wasn't her fault."

Alec nodded and then inquired, "What did Hillary do when she realized she had no other options?"

Leanne shrugged, "Nothing. I guess she decided she could handle him herself once the shock wore off."

Alec, always suspicious, wondered whether *handle* meant kill. Keeping that to himself, he remarked, "I'm glad he didn't get a chance to ruin the vacations of Irena's other guests."

The doctor agreed but then offered, "He was his own worst enemy. I did what I could for him, but I've learned that life doesn't always work out the way you want it to." Taking his wife's hand, he resumed. "We've had our share of heartaches."

The food came seconds later and after the server deposited fish and chips in front of the men and lobster rolls before the women, everyone tucked into their meals. Over a second round of drinks, Paige brought up the Bishops and asked Leanne, "If my aunt sells the B&B to Joan would you still be as interested in staying at the inn?"

Leanne glanced at her husband and answered for them. "I think so, as long as the food remains as good, and the rates remain competitive. We like Joan and Patrick is adorable. After meeting Richard Cassidy in the flesh, it's really amazing that Patrick turned out so well."

The DunBarton's evening was just as pleasant as their afternoon. Teatime went smoothly and Irena accepted Joan's invitation to have dinner at her house. Since Patrick volunteered to run over in case of an emergency, Alec decided it would be the perfect time to woo Paige. In his eyes, they were still newlyweds.

For dinner, Alec ordered his wife's favorite takeout dishes from a local Chinese restaurant. He was able to borrow a set of candles and a tablecloth from Irena earlier that afternoon and had a bottle of red wine chilling in the suite's refrigerator. To complete the mood, Alec had the inn's television set tuned to a soft rock music station.

Paige, who had been luxuriating in the whirlpool tub, came out of the bathroom to learn that dinner was being served on the outside balcony table. Paige only had time to run a comb through her hair and wrap a terrycloth robe around herself.

The night air was a perfect temperature, and Paige was delighted to see Alec's dinner laid out on the candlelit tablecloth. Alec behaving like a trained sommelier, with a napkin draped over his arm, pulled out his wife's chair. As he opened the bottle of wine in front of her and poured a small amount in her glass, he asked, "Madame, is it to your liking?"

Taking part in the fun, Paige swirled the red liquid in the glass, inhaled its aroma, and took a sip, letting the wine linger in her mouth. After swallowing it, she pronounced, "It's exquisite. You can pour me a full glass."

"Very good, Madame," Alec replied. "Since you appear to be alone, would you mind if I joined you for dinner?"

Paige indicated that he should take a seat but warned, "My husband can be a very jealous man."

"For such a lovely lady, I'll take my chances." Alec proceeded to open the carton of white rice and the plastic trays containing pork spareribs, chicken with broccoli, and shrimp in garlic sauce.

Once their plates were filled, Alec resumed his role of husband and detective and asked, "Did you learn anything interesting from Leanne Pierce today?"

Nibbling on her sparerib, Paige remarked, "She seemed a lot happier today and less distracted. Leanne and Alan had a great time at Camden yesterday. She also told me that Hillary is going to see our handsome police chief again. I think tomorrow. Did you get anything out of Dr. Pierce?"

Alec shook his head. "Not much. He was able to tell me what happens to a human body when people experience anaphylactic shock. The mild symptoms include hives, itching, and flushed skin. Some people may stop breathing when their tongue swells and their airways constrict.

"Further complications set in when patients are over fifty and their blood pressure plummets. In Cassidy's case, the shock caused him to go into cardiac arrest. From what Alan told me, it appears he did everything humanly possible to save him."

The couple continued to chat about their day until the sun dipped below the horizon. Even though it had become cooler, Paige wanted to remain outside. After clearing the table, Alec rejoined Paige with an extra comforter from inside their suite.

Alec wrapped it around his wife and then poured himself a scotch. Neither had to say a word. Paige was content to rest her head against her husband's chest on their oversized chaise lounge while he sipped his after-dinner drink.

When Paige's nose began to get cold and tingle from the night air, she suggested, "I think it's time for us to go in. I'll need you to warm me up."

Alec didn't have to be told twice.

He followed his wife into their suite and when she removed her terrycloth robe and slipped under the covers, he was right behind her.

CHAPTER TEN

▼

"Sailing"
Words & Music by Christopher Cross
Genre: Soft Rock, Released: June 1980

Saturday Morning—9th of July

Alec and Paige had a light morning. When they showed up in the kitchen, they not only found Irena but also Joan Bishop preparing breakfast. Joan was attired in an apron and busily removing eggs, cream, smoked salmon, and scallions from the refrigerator.

Smiling from ear to ear, Irena announced, "Joan is going to buy the inn from me when Patrick inherits his father's money. Joan thinks Cassidy's estate, including his house, is worth over two million dollars. It might take a year for the estate to go through probate, but I don't mind.

"In the meantime, I'm going to teach Joan how to make all my scrumptious breads and cakes. She's going to help us in the kitchen three or four times a week and run the inn while the three of us are on the twelve-day cruise in northern Europe. Without her, I would have never been able to get away this August."

Irena's enthusiasm was catchy. Despite a momentary concern that their plans could fall through, Alec was thrilled to hear the good news. In fact, their cruise was scheduled to leave from Copenhagen, Denmark, on the ninth, which was exactly one month away.

With Joan's help, Alec was able to get the Honey Spice Cake into the oven early. After Paige finished serving the bed and breakfast guests, the Bishops, the DunBartons, Karine, and Irena all congregated in the breakfast room to have a champagne toast and some leftover breakfast.

Karine was especially relieved to hear the news. She had been worried about Irena's health and didn't want to see her deal with the continual stress of running an inn.

When Joan announced that Irena was going to move into the Bishop's two-bedroom cottage and be on hand to help with baking and gardening, Irena interjected, "Since my fall, I've realized I need to live on one level. Joan's house will be plenty big for me, and once Patrick goes off to college, my cozy third floor apartment will be perfect for Joan."

It was obvious from their stated plans that Irena had been able to iron out an equitable agreement with Joan while she dined with her the previous evening. Patrick's face was brimming with pride as he refilled the champagne glasses and said, "To quote Miss Prism from *The Importance of Being Ernest*, 'The good ended happily, and the bad unhappily.'"

Paige embraced her aunt, "I'm so happy for you! I know all your past bed and breakfast guests will be glad to still see you. Family isn't only composed of blood relatives. It's also made up of good friends and neighbors who help each other and are there for you during the tough times."

The champagne ran out all too fast, and Patrick had to excuse himself to check out the middle-aged couple from California. Before Karine could depart to clean the newly vacated room, Joan whispered in her ear, "I will need you more than ever and plan to raise your pay." Upon hearing that news, Karine nearly danced out of the breakfast room.

When the foursome was alone, Irena turned to Alec and said, "Paige told me you're a controller on the cruise ship and are quite clever with money. Would you mind looking over the agreement that Joan and I come to before we send it to a lawyer?"

Alec immediately agreed. Although he trusted Irena's instincts and Joan's motives, Alec felt he could do the most good by making sure that Irena was going to have a peaceful and happy retirement.

When the kitchen was clean and the Honey Spice Cake was cooling on the wire rack for afternoon tea, the group went their separate ways—Irena and Joan to go over their weekly revenue and the DunBartons to go on their first boat excursion in Boothbay Harbor.

Wearing sunhats and sunscreen, the DunBartons departed for the harbor pier to collect the tickets that Alec had ordered online from Cap'n Fish's Cruises. After speaking to a young fellow at the kiosk, he confirmed they were registered on the captain's one-thirty cruise and had to merely show up at Pier 1 by 1:15 PM. On the three-hour trip, they were going to see lighthouses and seals, and also learn how to haul in a lobster trap from the bay.

Assured of a spot on the boat, Alec looked at his watch and pronounced, "We have an hour to kill. Do you want to get a quick lunch?"

Paige was about to answer when she realized that Alec was no longer there. Following his nose as usual, he was steps ahead of her and at the door of Pier 1 Pizza. The eatery was busy with people waiting to order and those eager to collect their food. Alec was reading from the posted menu when Paige joined him and said, "I guess you're going to have a few slices."

While Alec ordered two Margherita slices for himself and a vegetable for his wife, Paige hurried outside to look for an empty picnic table in front of the Windjammer Emporium. Alec stopped by just long enough to drop off two diet colas, promising to return. Ten minutes later, he was back with paper plates laden with hot, cheesy pizza.

It didn't take long for the DunBartons to finish their meal. Even though it was only one o'clock, Alec observed, "People are already lining up at the pier. I guess we'd better, too. I want to get a good seat on the upper deck."

Alec and Paige waited in the queue for fifteen minutes. The sun was stronger than they had anticipated, and the pair was happy when the boat crew opened the gate to the ramp and started to let people board. Alec maneuvered Paige up the boat's staircase and to the deck's first row. From their vantage point on the port side, they were able to see a large number of boats moored on their left.

Paige grew excited as they waited for the boat to take on all of its passengers, and commented, "I can't remember the last time I was on a boat."

Alec was about to make a wisecrack about living on a cruise ship when the boat's tour guide announced on the overhead speakers, "We'll be setting off in a few minutes. The passenger life vests are located above the benches on the lower level and under the seats on the top deck. If anyone wants refreshments, Pete is at the refreshment bar ready to take your orders for coffee, soda, hot chocolate, and snacks."

Surprised, Paige exclaimed, "I can't imagine we're going to want hot chocolate. I'm still uncomfortably warm."

Alec chuckled when the boat backed up and they found themselves in the shade. As the boat pulled away from the harbor and the breeze grew stronger, Paige shivered and muttered, "I'm sorry I ever said anything."

The tour guide's voice was clear and loud while she pointed out places of interest and explained their significance. To Alec's right was a small island with pine trees that was owned by one family who summered there. To his left was Carousel Marina, where the movie *Carousel* was filmed in 1956. Some Boothbay Harbor residents had been extras in the famous musical.

As the boat slowly maneuvered between colorful buoys that bobbed on the water's surface, the guide announced, "In Maine, we have about six thousand fishermen and women who are licensed to catch lobsters. Lobster trappers have buoys that are unique to them. The buoys are connected by rope to the traps on the ocean floor. The color and design of the buoys must match the markings on the lobster person's boat, so authorities can tell whether a lobsterman is removing his own catch.

"Lobstermen work long hours, often in severe weather. They need to be fit enough to lift forty-pound traps out of the ocean and be able to navigate the fishing grounds, bait their traps, and locate and catch a large number of crustaceans. The season runs from May to December. You'll learn more about lobsters and the fishermen who catch them when we return to the harbor. Meanwhile, sit back and relax. The boat will speed up after we pass the Spruce Point Inn and clear most of these lobster buoys."

Alec removed his sunhat in order to feel the wind in his hair. Despite the presence of sightseers behind him, Alec crooned,

Well, it's not far down to paradise, at least it's not for me
And if the wind is right, you can sail away and find tranquility
Oh, the canvas can do miracles, just you wait and see
Believe me

It's not far to never-never land, no reason to pretend
And if the wind is right, you can find the joy of innocence again
Oh, the canvas can do miracles, just you wait and see
Believe me

Sailing takes me away to where I've always heard it could be
Just a dream and the wind to carry me
And soon I will be free

Fantasy, it gets the best of me
When I'm sailing
All caught up in the reverie, every word is a symphony
Won't you believe me?

Sailing takes me away to where I've always heard it could be
Just a dream and the wind to carry me
And soon I will be free

Well it's not far back to sanity, at least it's not for me
And if the wind is right, you can sail away and find serenity
Oh, the canvas can do miracles, just you wait and see
Really, believe me

Sailing takes me away to where I've always heard it could be
Just a dream and the wind to carry me
And soon I will be free

Paige turned around to see if anyone had objected to Alec's singing and only saw the faces of happy people as their bodies swayed in sync with the waves.

The boat slowed as it neared the Burnt Island Lighthouse. From the guide, the DunBartons learned that the working lighthouse was built in 1821 and sat on a five-acre island, approximately one mile from the center of Boothbay Harbor. Though summer visitors, teachers, and school children were welcome to tour the historic lighthouse, it could only be reached by boat.

After passing the secluded island, Paige muttered, "Can you imagine what it was like to operate the lighthouse in the 1800s on cold, foggy nights?"

Alec kissed his wife's forehead and whispered, "I would have found a way to keep you warm, Lass."

Paige shivered from the cool air that rushed past them and Alec had to move closer to share his body warmth.

On the way to the next lighthouse, the guide called their attention to seals basking on the rocks of a barren island. While Paige and Alec took pictures, the other sightseers oohed and aahed as they watched the harbor seals dive into the water and waddle back onto the craggy land.

The next stop was the Ram Island Lighthouse. It was built in 1837 when seafarers agreed it was needed and implored Congress to appropriate five thousand dollars to purchase it. The island was originally used to quarantine rams and control the breeding of sheep. The lighthouse was automated in 1965 and slowly fell victim to vandalism until 2002 when the building and the keeper's house were restored.

The trip back to town was equally relaxing. After purchasing a cup of hot chocolate, Paige finally warmed up and was able to let the sun's rays touch her exposed skin. As the boat drew closer to Boothbay Harbor, it slowed and stopped by a buoy.

When two deck hands moved to the bow of the boat, the tour guide announced, "We're going to give you some background information on Maine's famous lobster industry."

She continued, "Mark is using the hand over hand motion to bring the lobster trap up from the ocean floor. Gary is helping him place the metal lobster trap onto the deck. Lobster traps have not changed much over the last two hundred years. The entrance of a trap is designed to only let lobsters in. Undersized crustaceans can crawl out through smaller exit holes."

Paige moved closer to the boat's railing to observe the young men below, They removed the squirming lobsters from the trap and held them up. The guide explained that in Maine the minimum legal size was 3¼ inches and the maximum was 5 inches. Lobsters were measured from their rear eye socket to the beginning of their tail. "Shorts" and over-sized lobsters were to be thrown back.

When Mark showed the observers, a lobster with soft, feathery appendages under its tail, the guide resumed. "Mark is holding up a female lobster. Females that are carrying eggs under their tails must be notched with a V in their flipper to show they are breeders. These lobsters must be returned to the sea, and a lobsterman who keeps a V-notched lobster can be fined upwards of a thousand dollars."

Alec grunted. "I can understand why they toss back breeders, but a thousand dollars sounds pretty steep to me. I wonder how much a lobsterman can make."

Although the narrator couldn't hear the DunBartons, Alec was surprised to hear her say, "Lobstermen and women have a number of expenses. Along with fuel and equipment, the price of lobster bait has risen. Upon returning to shore, fishermen have their daily catch weighed at the lobster wharf. There can be days when their expenses outweigh their income."

After the empty trap was refilled with fresh bait and lowered into the water, the boat headed back to the town's pier. While the passengers were disembarking, Alec remarked to Paige, "I can now appreciate how hard Karine's husband must work to make a good living. I wonder whether Cassidy really saw Mr. Rybakov cut a lobster line belonging to a fellow trapper."

"If lobstermen can be fined and lose their license for cutting another person's line," Paige responded. "I could see them paying blackmail or worse."

"Worse?" Alec echoed.

"Permanently getting rid of the nasty blackmailer!"

CHAPTER ELEVEN

▼

"She's Always A Woman"
Words & Music by Billy Joel
Genre: Soft Rock, Released: July 1977

Saturday Afternoon—9th of July

Alec and Paige returned to the inn at five o'clock. Alec was grateful that Joan and Irena had been on hand to serve afternoon tea to a pair of sisters from Albany, New York. The newcomers were happily settled in the Windward Room and were finding a lot to talk about with the chatty woman staying in the Portside Room.

Since Joan and Irena were not in a rush to clean up the parlor, Alec asked, "Would you mind if Paige and I take a quick shower. The boat ride was wonderful, but we feel like we've been baked in the sun and seasoned with salt."

Irena smiled. "Go right ahead and relax. I defrosted chop meat and buns for tonight. When you and Paige get hungry, come down and we'll grill some burgers."

Paige thanked her aunt with a kiss to her soft cheek and then rushed up the stairs toward their suite. Alec was right behind her, aware that he'd have to give his wife first dibs in the shower. Although Paige was a very generous woman, he was not going to come between her and soapy hot water.

Alec could see that Paige had not wasted a moment. Her clothes were strewn on the floor, and she had not completely closed the front door of Mariner's Retreat. Certain she was going to be in the shower for a while, Alec helped himself to a hefty portion of Glenlivet and stepped onto the balcony.

Paige joined him twenty minutes later with freshly washed hair and adorned in a loose-fitting sundress. Despite being hot and then cold on the boat, she pointed out, "My face and arms have gotten sunburned. I hope I don't peel later."

"Even when you're peeling, you look beautiful," Alec replied. "Can I get you something to drink? The sun is also dehydrating."

Taking a sip from his glass, Paige wrinkled her nose. "I wouldn't mind a nice refreshing gin and tonic."

Alec returned with an ice-filled glass to find Paige stretched out on the comfy chaise lounge. Since her eyes were beginning to close, he placed the glass beside her on the cocktail table. After kissing her forehead, he whispered, "I'm going to bathe."

At seven, Alec awakened his wife with a smile. "You've been sleeping for an hour, and your aunt is too polite to demand our presence in the kitchen."

Paige hastened to her feet and saluted her husband. "Yes, sir."

The couple quickly descended the outdoor staircase to find Irena on the first-floor deck, using her one good arm to cook hamburgers and corn on the charcoal grill.

"You're right on time," she called and explained, "Patrick brought up the grill from the storage area and the briquettes from last year lit up right away."

Alec was amazed that Irena was still so full of vim and vigor, and acknowledged, "You're a marvel. I hope Paige and I have half your energy when we're your age."

Irena grinned while she instructed Alec to flip the burgers over. Paige and Irena left to make a salad and set a table in the breakfast room. When everything was grilled to perfection, Alec carried a platter of cheeseburgers with toasted buns and charred corn on the cob into the room.

Alec had not realized how hungry he was until he sat down to eat. After serving Irena and Paige, he helped himself. Paige's salad contained fresh produce that Karine had picked up earlier in the day. Everything was delicious.

The dinner conversation was lively. Irena related, "While you were showering, the Pierces returned from their outing to Monhegan Island. Their boat left Boothbay at 9:30 AM and they were pretty sunburned and exhausted when they came in at six. He ordered Chinese take-out for dinner, and I expect they're going to turn in early."

As Irena was taking a sip of lemonade, Paige asked, "Did they have a good time? I picked up brochures for that trip, a clambake at Cabbage Island, and a whale watching expedition. I don't know which one we should try next."

Irena nodded, "Monhegan Island is about eleven miles from here by ferry. I think the Pierces enjoyed it even though it takes about three hours to get there. Young people like to hike on the island's many trails, and artists go to paint landscapes and seascapes. No cars are allowed on the island. I always find the place a bit backward, and there's only one public bathroom on the island."

Surprised, Paige remarked, "That's good to know. We'll make sure to use the boat's facilities if we go."

Alec didn't think it sounded appealing and asked about Hillary. Luckily, the topic changed from toilets to romance as Irena shared, "Hillary went out on another dinner date with our handsome police chief. I've never seen her so nervous before. She tried on several outfits before finally settling on a dark green dress. They went to the Thistle Inn Restaurant which can be pretty pricey. He must really like her."

Paige agreed, "Those first few dates can be nerve wracking. When Alec asked me to have a drink with him on our first date, he grilled me for information."

"I did not!" Alec exclaimed and then corrected himself. "Initially, I may have suspected you of murder, but you were also the sexiest woman on the ship."

Affectionately, Paige patted Alec's arm and declared, "Hillary doesn't seem like a vulnerable sort of person to me."

Before Paige could add to that thought, Alec sang out

She can kill with a smile
She can wound with her eyes
She can ruin your faith with her casual lies
And she only reveals what she wants you to see
She hides like a child
But she's always a woman to me

She can lead you to love
She can take you or leave you
She can ask for the truth
But she'll never believe
And she'll take what you give her as long as it's free
Yeah, she steals like a thief
But she's always a woman to me

Oh, she takes care of herself
She can wait if she wants
She's ahead of her time
Oh, and she never gives out
And she never gives in
She just changes her mind

She will promise you more
Than the Garden of Eden
Then she'll carelessly cut you
And laugh while you're bleedin'
But she'll bring out the best
And the worst you can be
Blame it all on yourself
Cause she's always a woman to me

Oh, she takes care of herself
She can wait if she wants
She's ahead of her time
Oh, and she never gives out
And she never gives in
She just changes her mind

She is frequently kind
And she's suddenly cruel
She can do as she pleases
She's nobody's fool
But she can't be convicted
She's earned her degree
And the most she will do
Is throw shadows at you
But she's always a woman to me

Irena clapped after Alec finished his rendition of the Billy Joel song and agreed, "Those lyrics describe Hillary perfectly."

The threesome discussed the Bishops while having leftover Honey Spice Cake for dessert. Irena brought up Patrick first and mentioned, "The OCME released Cassidy's body today and had it sent to a funeral home on Wiscasset Road in Boothbay. Poor Patrick still doesn't know what to do with the judge's remains.

"When Officer Taylor came by to pick up Hillary, he gave Patrick the keys to the judge's house. Tomorrow, he and Joan plan to go over there. Hillary volunteered to accompany them on their walkthrough. She knows exactly what upgrades were made in the house and where everything is located."

Alec nodded. "Joan and Patrick better have the workers continue their black mold removal. The Bishops will get a better price for the property when they put the house on the market."

"Does Joan still want to scatter Cassidy's ashes in her garden?" Paige posed impishly. "It will eventually be your garden. And what do you plan to do with her bees?"

Irena winked. "I won't mind living with the judge's ashes or the bees. Just last Saturday, Dick Cassidy accused me of poisoning him with the honey in my spice cake. No, I won't mind walking on his remains!"

Alec was cleaning up the kitchen when he heard Walt and Hillary return to the inn. Quietly, he stepped into the breakfast room where he could watch the couple unobserved. After they ascended the stairs to the second-floor landing, Alec hurried over to the Sunrise Room.

Paige had just settled her aunt in the suite's king-sized bed for the night. Irena looked like a precious doll, sitting up against plush pillows and surrounded by a fluffy comforter. Paige eyed the area and pronounced, "Your wheelchair is to your left, and I put a glass of fresh water on your bedside table. Oh, and here's the TV remote."

Paige put the remote on her aunt's bedcovers as Irena replied, "You're spoiling me, dear. I'm really able to take care of myself. I don't always need the wheelchair. I can hobble around with my cane."

Before Alec could shoo Paige out the door, Irena reminded the DunBartons, "Tomorrow, the handyman is coming by to fix the spray hose on the kitchen sink. It's been leaking. And don't forget I have a doctor's appointment with the orthopedist on Monday. I've arranged for Joan to be here while we're out."

Alec promised, "We'll get you over to the doctor's office on time. I think he'll be amazed to see how well you're doing."

When their good nights were exchanged, Alec shut the door behind them and whispered to Paige, "Let's go upstairs. I want to see if we can hear some of the conversation between Walt and Hillary."

Paige scolded Alec, "You mean eavesdrop." Despite their difference of opinion, Paige followed him to their third-floor suite. Quickly, Alec stepped into the room and opened the sliding door to the balcony, hoping that the police chief and Hillary were sitting outside. Her room was directly under theirs.

Alec signaled for Paige to be silent and indicated for her to take a seat on the chaise next to him. Together, the DunBartons waited, and they were not disappointed.

The door below them made a slight noise as it slid open, and they heard Hillary invite Walt to take a seat on the outdoor deck furniture. Alec thought he could make out the sound of a bottle and glasses being placed on a cocktail table.

Walt's voice was rather low and husky, and he spoke at a slow pace. It was not easy to make out his words. Even though Hillary had a British accent, her speech pattern was clearer. Alec had no trouble following her end of their conversation.

Neither of them mentioned Richard Cassidy's death and when their tête-à-tête became more personal, Paige whispered to Alec, "That's enough!"

While Alec was tiptoeing back into their suite, he heard Walt groan and the sound of a female sigh.

After Paige closed their sliding door, she said to Alec, "It's obvious that Walt finds Hillary a very special woman."

CHAPTER TWELVE

▼

"This Is It"
Words & Music by Kenny Loggins and Michael McDonald
Genre: Soft Rock, Released: October 1979

Sunday Morning—10th of July

Alec couldn't wait to prepare breakfast. He jumped out of bed before Paige, which was out of character for him, and hurried to shower and shave. Rising from her side of the bed, Paige trudged into the bathroom and called to Alec, "What in the world has gotten into you?"

Poking his head out of the shower, Alec replied, "I have a 'special gift' that you know nothing about. I can tell by looking at a person's face whether he or she had sex the previous evening."

In response, Paige's mouth dropped open and when she was able to close it again, she merely said, "Posh and nonsense."

While drying off, Alec stuck to his guns and claimed, "You'll see!"

Paige had to hurry to catch up with her husband. It was 7:15 AM when the DunBartons entered the kitchen.

The menu for the day read:

Orange, Apple, and V8 Juice
Pork or Turkey Sausage
Swiss and Mushroom Quiche
Blueberry Blintz Souffle with Sour Cream
Date Nut Bread with Cream Cheese

Alec started on the souffle first since it needed to bake for an hour and fifteen minutes. While he was popping it into the oven, Paige gathered the ingredients for the quiche together. It included: ready-made pie crust, eggs, cream, half and half, mushrooms, spinach, and a block of Swiss cheese. Everything was going smoothly until Alec started to shred the cheese on a four-sided metal grater.

All of a sudden, Alec cried out in pain. There was blood on the grater's surface and red droplets on the creamy cheese. Alec immediately rushed to the sink to rinse off his palm and look at his injury.

The abrasion was hard to see as blood kept rushing out of his wound. After instructing Alec to press a dishcloth on the laceration and hold his arm above his head, Paige rushed out of the kitchen.

Alec still had his hand raised when Paige returned with Dr. Pierce, carrying his medical case. It looked as though Paige had awakened him. Alan's hair was ruffled, and his robe was untied over his pajamas. Alan took charge and said, "Let me see what damage you've done to the quiche."

Paige started to laugh, and Alec showed the doctor his palm. The bleeding had stopped, and he could make out a few grater-sized lacerations.

Pierce opened his medical bag and took out cleanser, antiseptic ointment, sterile gauze, and adhesive bandages. The doctor was just finishing his handiwork when Irena rolled herself into the kitchen, followed by Leanne.

Irena wanted to know what had happened. After fussing over Alec, she had Paige throw out the bloody shredded cheese and wash the grater.

Gratefully, Alec thanked the doctor and turned down his offer of painkillers and a tetanus shot. Even though the cuts weren't deep, Pierce suggested, "Take it easy this morning and let me know if it starts to bleed again, swells, or discharges pus."

While glancing at the physician's black case, sitting on the silverware counter, Alec remarked, "I'm glad you still carry a medical bag. My father is a retired doctor in Scotland and doesn't go anywhere without his."

Alan agreed. "I'm afraid they've gone out of style with the younger doctors. It came in handy when the judge needed a second EpiPen injection. I'm just sorry it didn't help."

Leanne helped Paige finish the Swiss Cheese Quiche while Irena served Alec and Alan a cup of hot coffee in the breakfast room. When the doctor departed, Irena returned to the kitchen to check on how the women were doing.

The rest of the breakfast preparations went without a hitch. The doctor returned to the breakfast room at nine o'clock, dressed for the day and eager to have some of *his wife's* quiche. The other guests arrived hungry and also enjoyed their morning selections.

It was nearly ten when Hillary Fairchild wandered in for a late breakfast. She was smiling from ear to ear and Alec decided his "special gift" was functioning properly.

While Patrick was out with his mother and Hillary, Paige filled in at the front desk. Alec was able to make the Chocolate Chip Dream Bars by himself, careful not to apply unnecessary pressure against his injured palm.

Alec was finished by the time Chip arrived. Although the handyman got right down to business fixing the kitchen faucet spray hose, Alec found his incessant chatter annoying. Chip Granger considered himself a Don Juan with the women in town. Wondering whether Joan Bishop had ever been one of Chip's conquests, Alec asked him.

Chip stopped what he was doing and answered, "We had a short fling two years ago, She fell for me hook, line, and sinker when I repaired a portion of her leaking roof. It was a hot day, and

I had to remove my shirt. I know she liked my muscular chest and the way the sweat dripped off it."

Alec grimaced at his description and posed, "How long did you two go out?"

Chip looked as though he was casting his mind back and then answered, "A week or two."

Alec wasn't surprised. Joan, if she had really succumbed to his overtures, was too smart to spend any time with Chip. The fellow was immature and exhibited attention-seeking behavior. It remained to be seen whether he was a good handyman.

When Paige called Alec from the front desk to help the chatty woman move the luggage from her suite to her car, he hopped to it. Alec was glad to get away from Chip. He was even happier to return to the inn's foyer with a twenty-dollar bill that the woman had stuffed in his hand.

Paige sighed in response and sent Alec to help Karine clean up the newly vacated room.

From the housekeeper, Alec learned that an elderly couple was going to check into Portside Retreat at three o'clock, and the Pierces planned to check out the following morning. Alec had mixed feelings about the Pierce's coming departure. He liked both Alan and Leanne but didn't want anyone to leave the inn until he was sure that Cassidy's death was an accident.

The inn remained quiet until 4:00 PM. Alec and Paige set up the parlor like old pros and all the afternoon tea paraphernalia were set out on time. Alan and Leanne were the first to arrive.

Chip, who had found more things to fix in the kitchen, came in after them. The Bishops and Hillary followed. Patrick was gleeful about the valuable items he'd found in his father's house, and Joan hurried to the sofa, exhausted from walking all over Cassidy's property. Hillary, still glowing from her evening's activities, found a seat beside Joan.

While everyone was helping themselves to the Chocolate Chip Dream Bars and hot tea, Irena and Karine joined the group. The housekeeper wanted to personally say goodbye to the Pierces and wish them a safe trip back to Vermont in case she didn't see them in the morning.

It occurred to Alec that the parlor was filled with the same people who had been together on July fourth when Richard Cassidy died. Alec took a moment to look at each of the occupants.

Paige was sitting next to her aunt with a loving expression on her face. Karine was discussing something with Chip, and Joan was speaking to Leanne about the judge's home furnishings. Hillary was texting a message on her phone, and Alan looked as though he was about to fall asleep in the easy chair.

Leanne must have noticed that her husband's head was slumped to one side and said, "I have to finish packing, and it looks like Alan needs to take a nap."

Alec felt a bit guilty. It was his mishap in the kitchen that had robbed the doctor of a full night's sleep. Karine left minutes after the Pierces to get dinner on the stove for her husband, and the Bishops, a half hour later to contact a real estate agency.

Chip was reminded by Irena to come back in a week to weed the garden and cut the grass. Upon stuffing some bar cookies in his pocket, "for the road," Chip departed. The remaining threesome cleaned up the parlor and put away the dishes.

Alec was about to sit down and relax on the first-floor deck when he heard a woman shriek. Back inside, Alec was surprised to see Leanne on the staircase with her face contorted in fear. When she was able to speak, she cried, "I can't wake up Alan! Hurry, call an ambulance."

Paige called for one while Alec took the steps upstairs, two at a time.

Dr. Pierce was fully dressed, except for his shoes, and stretched out on top of the bed. Alec tried to awaken him. But, no matter how vigorously he shook him, the doctor remained still. Alec was about to listen for his heartbeat when the EMS arrived.

The paramedics got right to work on him checking his pulse, oxygen level, respiratory rate, and heart function. A team member asked Alec, "Did he take anything? Is there anything in this room that could have harmed him? Was he complaining of any physical discomfort?" Alec was unable to tell them much other that he had a cup of Earl Grey tea an hour earlier and seemed pretty sleepy.

Leanne sobbed while the ambulance personnel brought her husband down the stairs on a stretcher. She wanted to go with them in the ambulance, but Paige suggested, "Let the EMS workers do everything they can. It's better you don't get in their way. We can go directly to the hospital in our car."

Alec didn't like leaving Irena alone and made her promise to call the Bishops if anything arose that she couldn't handle. The ambulance took off shortly later for Lincoln Health Hospital, Miles Campus, in Damariscotta.

Paige was able to calm Leanne down and got her settled in the backseat of Irena's car as Alec slipped into the driver's seat. The ride took exactly 27 minutes. When they arrived at the emergency department, the threesome was told that a doctor was with Alan and to take a seat in the waiting room.

Alec had the wherewithal to keep his mouth shut and found himself silently singing the lyrics,

There've been times in my life
I've been wonderin' why
Still, somehow, I believed we'd always survive
Now, I'm not so sure
You're waiting here
One good reason to try
But what more can I say
What's left to provide

You think that maybe it's over
Only if you want it to be
Are you gonna wait for a sign, your miracle
Stand up and fight

(This is it)
Make no mistake where you are
(This is it)
Your back's to the corner
(This is it)

Don't be a fool anymore
(This is it)

The waiting is over, no, don't you run
No way to hide
No time for wonderin' why
It's here, the moment is now, about to decide
Let 'em believe
Leave 'em behind
But keep me near in your heart
Know whatever you do
I'm here by your side

You say that maybe it's over
Not if you don't want it to be
For once in your life
Here's your miracle
Stand up and fight

(This is it)
Make no mistake where you are
(This is it)
You're goin' no further
(This is it)
Until it's over and done

It was an hour later when the emergency doctor had a nurse fetch Leanne. She wanted Alec and Paige to stay with her and gave the doctor permission to speak in front of them.

The doctor, a middle-aged balding man, cleared his throat and began, "You're husband is stable now. He overdosed on a mixture of opioids and benzodiazepines. Do you know whether he was taking either of those drugs?"

Leanne shook her head in the negative but acknowledged, "There had been times in the past he had been on oxycodone for a brief period. He knew the dangers of taking opioids for any length of time and that it should never be taken with anxiety medicine. As to the antidepressants, Alan never used them."

"I believe your husband is a primary care physician," the doctor cited. "If he didn't take the pills accidently or on purpose, is it possible that someone slipped them to him?"

Alec replied for Leanne. "This morning I had a minor accident in the kitchen and Dr. Pierce patched me up. I can't recall if he took his medical bag with him when he returned to his suite."

Leanne glanced at Paige before answering, "I think we left it on the kitchen counter. Oh my, do you think someone tried to poison him?"

The emergency doctor continued, "You may need to contact the local police in Boothbay Harbor. At the hospital, Dr. Pierce was injected with naloxone to counteract the opioid and flumazenil to offset the benzodiazepines.

"I'm going to keep him in the hospital overnight and possibly tomorrow to monitor him for seizures. You got your husband to the hospital just in time. When we get his toxicology results on Tuesday, we'll know just how close he came to dying in the ambulance."

Leanne asked if she could see her husband for a few minutes and was told to make it short. While she was away, Paige voiced her concerns and said, "I'll need to find another room for Leanne to stay in while Alan is recuperating."

Alec had other things on his mind. First, was Dr. Pierce poisoned with pills taken from his own medical kit? Second, did his poisoner try to silence the doctor because he knew who killed Richard Cassidy and how it was done?

CHAPTER THIRTEEN

▼

"White Rabbit"
Words & Music by Grace Slick
Genre: Psychedelic Rock, Released: June 1967

Sunday Evening—10th of July

Alec, Paige, and Leanne returned to the inn at 8:30 PM. Irena was full of questions and had some sandwiches waiting for the DunBartons and Mrs. Pierce. Leanne wasn't very hungry and took one up to her room to have later.

As she was mounting the steps with the plate in her hand, she turned around in shock and cried, "Do you have anywhere I can stay while Alan is in the hospital?"

Immediately, Irena squashed her fears. Taking a list from the side pocket of her wheelchair, Irena advised, "I have that all figured out. While you were at the hospital, I rearranged a few bookings. I'll have Patrick move you to the Windward Room tomorrow. You can stay there for two or three nights and if you need more time, we can move you back to the Starboard Suite."

Leanne thanked her for her hospitality and continued up the steps with a weary expression.

Paige, equally grateful, looked over her aunt's shoulder to see the room changes. It read:

		Sunrise Room #1	Windward Room #2	Starboard Suite #3	Portside Retreat #4	Harbor Escape #5	Mariner's Retreat #6
Fri	1	I. Anderson	R. Cassidy	A. Pierce	K. Stone	G. Castrovilla	Renovated
Sat	2	I. Anderson	R. Cassidy	A. Pierce	K. Stone	H. Fairchild	Renovated
Sun	3	I. Anderson	R. Cassidy	A. Pierce		H. Fairchild	A. DunBarton
Mon	4	I. Anderson	R. Cassidy	A. Pierce	S. Frisch	H. Fairchild	A. DunBarton
Tue	5	I. Anderson		A. Pierce	S. Frisch	H. Fairchild	A. DunBarton
Wed	6	I. Anderson		A. Pierce	S. Frisch	H. Fairchild	A. DunBarton
Thu	7	I. Anderson	K. Seidman	A. Pierce	N. Weaver	H. Fairchild	A. DunBarton
Fri	8	I. Anderson	K. Seidman	A. Pierce	N. Weaver	H. Fairchild	A. DunBarton
Sat	9	I. Anderson	J. Barnes	A. Pierce	N. Weaver	H. Fairchild	A. DunBarton
Sun	10	I. Anderson	J. Barnes	A. Pierce	L. Moody	H. Fairchild	A. DunBarton
Mon	11	I. Anderson	A. Pierce	R. Bayer	L. Moody	H. Fairchild	A. DunBarton
Tue	12	I. Anderson	A. Pierce	R. Bayer	B. Lambros	H. Fairchild	A. DunBarton
Wed	13	I. Anderson		R. Bayer	B. Lambros	H. Fairchild	A. DunBarton
Thu	14	I. Anderson	H. Beveridge		B. Lambros	M. Barton	A. DunBarton
Fri	15	I. Anderson	H. Beveridge		B. Lambros	M. Barton	A. DunBarton
Sat	16	I. Anderson	H. Beveridge	B. Jorgensen	R. Phelps	D. Jarrett	A. DunBarton
Sun	17	I. Anderson	H. Beveridge	B. Jorgensen	R. Phelps	D. Jarrett	A. DunBarton
Mon	18	I. Anderson		B. Jorgensen	R. Phelps	D. Jarrett	A. DunBarton
Tue	19	I. Anderson	L. Betts	M. Ackerman	T. Sikorski	D. Jarrett	A. DunBarton
Wed	20	I. Anderson	L. Betts	M. Ackerman	T. Sikorski		A. DunBarton
Thu	21	I. Anderson	L. Betts	D. Pavlenko		F. Harrell	A. DunBarton
Fri	22	D. Cruz	H. Gale	D. Pavlenko	K. Gibson	F. Harrell	A. DunBarton
Sat	23	D. Cruz	H. Gale	D. Pavlenko	K. Gibson	F. Harrell	A. DunBarton
Sun	24	D. Cruz		D. Pavlenko		W. Foss	A. DunBarton
Mon	25	D. Cruz	M. Kerrin	D. Pavlenko	C. Powers	W. Foss	A. DunBarton
Tue	26	D. Cruz	M. Kerrin		C. Powers		A. DunBarton
Wed	27			M. Miller	C. Powers	A. Hocking	A. DunBarton
Thu	28	B. Robinson	M. Conn	M. Miller	B. Morgan	A. Hocking	A. DunBarton
Fri	29	B. Robinson	M. Conn	M. Miller	B. Morgan	A. Hocking	A. DunBarton
Sat	30	B. Robinson	M. Conn	S. Cundiff	C. Montilli	A. Hocking	A. DunBarton
Sun	31	B. Robinson		S. Cundiff	C. Montilli	A. Hocking	A. DunBarton

Paige was surprised to see that her aunt planned to vacate her ground floor room on the 22nd of July and asked, "Do you think you'll be able to return to your apartment by then?"

Irena hurried Alec and Paige over to the breakfast room to have their meal while answering, "I'd better be. I hope the doctor will have good news for us tomorrow. In the meantime, I want to hear what happened at the hospital."

Alec filled her in while he and Paige hungrily ate their bacon, lettuce, and tomato sandwiches. Just as Alec was about to have a leftover Chocolate Chip Dream Bar, he heard the foyer door open.

Paige craned her neck around to see who was coming into the inn and called to the newcomers, "We're in the breakfast room."

As Hillary and Walt were entering the room, Officer Taylor remarked, "I heard you had some excitement tonight."

Alec was no longer surprised at how quickly news travelled in the small town of Boothbay Harbor. Hillary whispered something in Walt's ear and said her goodnights to the others.

After she departed for her suite, the police chief took a seat and pronounced, "The emergency room doctor at the hospital informed me that Dr. Pierce overdosed on pills this evening. From what I know of him, he's not the kind of man to take too many pills by accident or on purpose."

Alec agreed and then sang out,

> One pill makes you larger
> And one pill makes you small
> And the ones that mother gives you
> Don't do anything at all
> Go ask Alice
> When she's ten feet tall
>
> And if you go chasing rabbits
> And you know you're going to fall
> Tell 'em a hookah-smoking caterpillar
> Has given you the call
> Call Alice
> When she was just small
>
> When the men on the chessboard
> Get up and tell you where to go
> And you've just had some kind of mushroom
> And your mind is moving low
> Go ask Alice
> I think she'll know
>
> When logic and proportion
> Have fallen sloppy dead
> And the White Knight is talking backwards
> And the Red Queen's off with her head

Remember what the dormouse said
Feed your head
Feed your head

Though the song lyrics didn't help Alec ascertain whether Dr. Pierce knowingly took the pills, it did remind him to ask Walt whether he wanted a drug of a different kind and said, "Can I get you something alcoholic to drink?"

The chief consented with a nod while Paige fetched Alec's second bottle of Glenlivet, which was hidden in an upper cabinet in the kitchen. She not only came back with the whisky but also a box of food safety gloves and Pierce's medical bag, wrapped in a dish towel.

Alec chuckled. "My wife is fully versed in the dangers of contaminating evidence."

Paige placed the bag and gloves on the table while Irena fetched two clean glasses from the sideboard for their drinks. Once the men were served, Paige remarked to her aunt, "I think we'd better leave these two alone." As she pushed Irena's wheelchair out of the breakfast room, Paige added, "Don't stay up too late. I'm sure Walt has other things to do."

Walt didn't notice Paige's wink. After both men took a pair of disposable gloves from the box, the police chief carefully opened the bag's clasp and drew out a handwritten list. The list contained the names of the diagnostic equipment and the medications that were inside the bag.

It read:

Equipment:
Alcohol gel
Alcohol, wipes, gloves, lubricating jelly
Flashlight
Glucometer with strips and lancets
Multistix
Pocket Diagnostic Set

Prescription pad
Pulse oximeter
Reflex hammer
Sharps box
Specimen bottles and swabs
Sphygmomanometer cuff
Stethoscope
Syringes (2-1 milliliter, 2-2 milliliter, 2-5 milliliter)
Tongue depressor
Tourniquet

Medications:

Amoxicillin (125 mg/5 ml and 250 mg/5 ml oral suspension, 250mg capsules)
Aspirin (300 mg chewable tablets)
Atropine (600 micrograms/ml injection)
Benzylpenicillin (600 mg vials)
Codeine (25 mg in 5 ml syrup, 30 mg tablets)
Digoxin (750 microgram tablets)
Diazepam (5 mg tablets)
Epinephrine (1 mg/ml ampoules, 3 mg/ml auto injectors) Erythromycin (125 mg/5 ml and 250 mg/5 ml suspensions, 250 mg tablets)
Flumazenil (100 micrograms/ml injection)
Furosemide (10 mg/ml injection, 40 mg tablets
Glucagon (1 mg/ml injection)
Glyceryl trinitrate spray
Haloperidol (1.5 mg tablets, 5 mg/ml injections)
Hydrocortisone (100 mg powder)
Ibuprofen (100mg/5 ml oral suspension, 400 mg tablets)
Lorazepam (1 mg tablets, 4 mg/ml injection)
Morphine (10 mg/5 ml oral solution, 10mg/ml injection)
Naloxone (400 micrograms/ml injection)
Oral rehydration salt sachets
Prednisolone (20 mg tablets)

While Alec removed the equipment and medications from the bag, Walt marked off the name of the drug and the quantities of each from the list. Alec was flabbergasted at the amount of items that were contained in the small bag.

When the two men finished their drinks and their tasks, Alec looked over the list and announced, "You ticked everything off. Everything except the codeine, diazepam, and lorazepam tablets. I understand that opioids are extremely dangerous when taken with anxiety drugs in the benzodiazepine family."

Walt agreed, "Painkillers are extremely habit forming. Did Dr. Pierce have any old injuries that might have caused him to be in constant pain?"

Alec shook his head. "He seemed pretty spry to me and had no trouble getting around. The doctor also seemed happier the last few days. If he wanted to kill himself, why would he take pills when he had stronger injectable drugs in the medical bag to do the job?"

The police chief refilled his glass to its halfway mark and questioned, "Who had access to the medical kit today?"

Alec enumerated, "Chip, Karine, the Pierces, the Bishops, Hillary, Irena, Paige, and me."

Walt grimaced, "The whole gang!" Swallowing his scotch in one gulp, the officer grumbled, "It had better not be Hillary. I'm falling for her, and I've promised to tuck her into bed tonight."

With that said, Walt departed, and Alec smiled in spite of how the officer's feelings could impact the investigation.

Breakfast preparation went smoothly. Joan Bishop was on hand to help Alec in the kitchen. Both Bishops were amazed to hear that Dr. Pierce was in the hospital, and he had overdosed on a mixture of codeine and diazepam.

Joan was versed on the effects of both drugs and commented, "That combo is often used by people who are terminally ill. A few years ago, Maine passed a Death with Dignity Act that allows state residents, who are expected to die within six months, to obtain an oral prescription of medication to end their lives. Irena and I were very opposed to the bill's passage. Why, I wouldn't even kill my bees off if their days were numbered. Everyone and everything in life serves a purpose!"

Irena heard the last words of Joan's vehement statement and added, "I may not go to church regularly, but I agree with Joan. It's wrong to kill yourself. A person's pain is only momentary. We're all connected, and when a person dies before his or her time, it leaves a void in the lives of people around them. I believe God is the only one who can see the whole picture. We mustn't interfere with His plans and what He wants us to accomplish on earth."

Paige kissed her aunt's cheek and murmured, "You're very wise. There were times in my life, I've wondered whether I should be doing more than selling future cruise packages to well-to-do passengers. Now, when Alec and I solve crimes, we bring closure to the families of murder victims and see that former suspects can resume their lives blemish free."

Somberly, Alec confided, "When I lost Shanna and my daughter, Emma, to a drunk driver, I felt my life was never going to improve." Placing his arm around Paige, he added, "If I had tried to end it all then, I wouldn't have a beautiful new wife beside me now. I agree that God has something special for all of us to do."

Lightening the mood, Irena remarked, "I'm especially thrilled to have a handsome Scotsman cooking in my kitchen!"

Their mutual admiration society ended when Karine entered the breakfast room with Leanne. From the housekeeper's expression, Alec could tell she'd heard about Dr. Pierce's condition. After greeting them both, Paige asked Leanne how she was feeling.

Leanne looked a lot better than she appeared the night before. Her cheeks had color and her eyes were livelier. While Paige was serving her coffee, Leanne reported, "I slept well and woke up later than usual. I don't think I realized how tired I was. I spoke to the hospital this morning and the doctor is going to release Alan this afternoon as long as he promises to rest for the next few days."

Gazing at Irena, Leanne continued, "I'm so thankful you found a place for us to stay for the next two nights. I'm sure Alan's doctor won't mind if we head home on Wednesday morning."

When Leanne mentioned "doctor," Irena reminded Alec and Paige that her appointment to see the orthopedic surgeon was at noon. Since his office was located at Lincoln Health Hospital in Damariscotta, Alec asked Leanne whether she would need a lift to see her husband.

Leanne assured him that she could drive herself and would probably visit Alan once she was moved into the Windward Room and had some of their things unpacked. Patrick had already checked out the two sisters from Albany, and Karine promised to have the room ready by eleven. With everything planned, Alec, Paige, and Irena started to get ready for their outing.

CHAPTER FOURTEEN

▼

"Doctor, My Eyes"

Words & Music by Jackson Browne
Genre: Soft Rock, Released: March 1972

Monday Afternoon—11th of July

Alec had no trouble finding his way to Irena's orthopedic surgeon since he had just been to the hospital the day before. They arrived ten minutes early, which gave Alec enough time to remove the wheelchair from the car's trunk and get Irena settled onto the seat.

Irena scratched underneath her ankle cast and complained, "This thing had better come off today. It's been impossible to wash properly, and I feel so grubby!"

Paige commiserated with her as she wheeled Irena into the building. Their first stop was the radiology department where Irena was to have her ankle and wrist x-rayed. She was taken in right away. When the radiologist was happy with the film, Irena, Alec, and Paige were instructed to go to the doctor's office.

While in the surgeon's waiting room, the trio discussed Dr. Pierce and Alec asked, "Would you mind if I stopped off to see him after your appointment? I really need to know whether he tried to take his own life or overdosed by accident. If it wasn't one of those alternatives, there's a killer staying at the inn."

Irena shuddered but then replied, "You may not get an honest answer from Dr. Pierce. A failed suicide or drug overdose isn't something a person, especially a physician, is likely to admit."

Alec agreed but insisted, "I may be able to tell whether he's telling the truth by his countenance."

Their conversation was cut short when Irena was called next by a staff member.

The threesome followed the attendant into a small office where Irena was told to sit on the examining table. Alec had to help Paige's aunt onto the raised surface before the nurse could take her blood pressure, heart rate, and oxygen level. After Irena answered several questions, the nurse withdrew promising that the doctor would be in shortly.

The orthopedic surgeon entered five minutes later. He had a pleasant manner, asking not only medical questions but also how she was dealing with both injuries. The doctor examined her left wrist first and removed her soft cast. As he gently maneuvered her ligaments, he asked, "Does this hurt, and how much pain do you feel on a scale of one to five?"

After consulting her recent wrist x-ray on a computer screen, the doctor pronounced, "You had a moderate, grade two sprain and it's healing well. I'm going to put Miss Anderson's wrist in a lighter brace that will allow more movement. If you notice any swelling, I want you to ice and elevate your wrist. You mustn't overdo."

While Irena nodded, Alec remarked, "We'll make sure she behaves."

The doctor smiled in response, possibly knowing that his patient was headstrong and then said, "Let's take a look at your ankle. I'm going to cut off the cast. If it's healing as well as the x-ray indicates, "I'm going to let you go home in a soft cast."

Everyone watched as he removed the cast with a saw that moved from side to side. The vibrations caused Irena to giggle, and she exclaimed, "I didn't think I was ticklish."

When her limb was exposed, the doctor examined it for range of motion and her pain level. Since her skin had not seen daylight for two weeks, it looked dry, pale, and flaky. Irena cried, "I hope it doesn't smell too bad!"

The orthopedist laughed and called for his nurse, explaining that she was going to train them on how Irena was to use a special ankle stabilizer with a figure-eight strap to support the ankle. She was to wear it while standing more than a few minutes or just going several steps in the house. He didn't want her to take the stairs yet and asked if she had access to a walker.

Irena said she did and asked, "Does that mean I can get out of this wheelchair and also take a hot shower?"

After hearing that she could bathe and use the walker to get around in the inn, she practically jumped off the examining table.

The physician gazed at Alec and muttered, "You have to watch her. I don't want to see Miss Anderson in my office before her next appointment."

For the remainder of the office visit, the DunBartons watched the nurse remove the brace from its box and showed them how it was to be applied and taken off Irena's foot. She also handed Irena a list of ankle exercises that she was to practice on her bed with the stabilizer off.

When they were comfortable with what Irena was permitted to do and not do, the nurse allowed them to head over to the receptionist to schedule her follow-up appointment. From there, the ladies decided to stop by the cafeteria for a celebratory cup of coffee and piece of cake. Upon seeing them settled in the cafe, Alec headed over to Dr. Pierce's private hospital room to find out how he was doing.

Alec was glad to see that Leanne had not yet arrived and Alan was alone. The doctor was in great spirits and apparently happy to see Alec. While taking an empty chair beside his bed, Alec asked him how he was feeling.

Alan replied, "Fine now. I'd like to thank you for helping Leanne and getting me to the hospital in time. I know you have questions for me, but I didn't self-administer those drugs. I'm quite aware of what they can do. I'd also like to think that no one gave me those drugs on purpose. I can't imagine that anyone hates me that much. Perhaps the tea cups got mixed up."

Alec hadn't thought of that, but it didn't seem likely. Although Earl Grey tea, with its strong taste of bergamot, could mask the taste of some substances, only Alan and Leanne had it at teatime. Hillary was a fan of Darjeeling, and the others had herbal and ordinary English breakfast tea.

For a moment, Alec wondered whether Leanne had tried to kill herself and accidentally gave her husband the wrong teacup. Despite being outwardly pleasant, Leanne seemed lonely. Changing the topic, Alec asked Alan when he expected to be released from the hospital.

Dr. Pierce didn't think it would be until late afternoon. Their conversation about Irena's recent visit to her surgeon was cut short when Leanne arrived. She seemed a bit frazzled and started to rearrange her husband's bedding. Realizing that he knew little about the Pierces, as well as the others who had witnessed Cassidy's death, Alec decided to Google them upon his return to the B&B.

Keeping that to himself, Alec made his excuses. He knew Irena was probably eager to go home and try out the new ankle brace along with her walker.

Alec, Paige, and Irena returned to the inn at one-thirty. They were greeted by Patrick and Joan. Both of whom were thrilled to see Irena out of her cast and wanted to know everything her orthopedic surgeon had said. Joan had prepared a light lunch for them and Alec, eager to conduct his research, made it through the meal before excusing himself.

On the balcony outside his suite, Alec opened his laptop. He had used his cell phone to keep in contact with friends and family but felt the computer was a better tool to explore the internet. With a writing pad and pen beside him, Alec keyed into the search bar, "Bennington, Vermont. Dr. Alan Pierce."

Before scanning the results, Alec sang out.

Doctor, my eyes have seen the years
And the slow parade of fears without crying
Now I want to understand

I have done all that I could
To see the evil and the good without hiding
You must help me if you can

Doctor, my eyes
Tell me what is wrong
Was I unwise to leave them open for so long

'Cause I have wandered through this world
And as each moment has unfurled
I've been waiting to awaken from these dreams
People go just where they will
I never noticed them until I got this feeling
That it's later than it seems

Doctor, my eyes
Tell me what you see
I hear their cries
Just say if it's too late for me

Doctor, my eyes
They cannot see the sky
Is this the prize
For having learned how not to cry

The lyrics confirmed to Alec that he was still baffled and full of questions. Was Cassidy murdered? Did someone try to kill Dr. Pierce? More intent than ever to find answers, Alec glanced at the websites that populated the screen.

Under Alan Pierce, Alec read about his training, years of service, and appointment hours. The physician had an office at Southwestern Vermont Medical Center, a ninety-nine-bed facility in Bennington. He was one of 130 physicians on its medical staff.

His biography mentioned that he went to medical school in South Carolina, was a resident at Beth Israel Medical Center in New York, and did a fellowship in its Pain Medicine and Palliative Care Department.

Alec was not surprised to see that Alan had worked overseas with Doctors Without Borders in the early eighties. It was obvious from the way Pierce spoke that he was once a humanitarian and had cared for people in underdeveloped countries. It was also clear that Pierce later became bored tending to his well-to-do patients in the United States.

When Alec widened his search, he learned that Mr. and Mrs. Pierce belonged to the Mt. Anthony Country Club, where Leanne served on a few committees.

On a sad note, the Bennington Banner contained a very old obituary stating that the Pierce's twenty-year-old daughter had died in a car accident while attending college, leaving two younger brothers and her parents. Alec decided that it was the unhappy past that Alan had referred to when they had a late lunch at Brady's.

After finding out all he could on the Pierces, Alec Googled Hillary Fairchild. There was quite a lot on her and her interior decorating business. Alec recognized some of the names of her famous clients. Alec found one article about a couple who sued her for "tearing up their home." The couple's house was located in Portland, Maine, and the case was later settled out of court for an undisclosed amount.

As to her personal life, Alec learned that Hillary's ex-husband was a hot-shot attorney. They had a nasty divorce, which was plastered all over the scandal sheets. According to the papers, he was caught cheating on Hillary with a younger woman from his law firm. Since their son was already grown, it had a minimal effect on him. The divorce was finalized five years ago, leaving Hillary an opportunity to date a multitude of single and wealthy bachelors.

For the Boothbay Harbor residents, Alec searched through the internet as well. There was nothing on Karine Rybakov. Her husband, however, was mentioned in the Boothbay Register when his lobster boat capsized in a storm after a rogue wave hit it. No one was injured and the boat was towed back to shore.

On the Bishops, Alec located a printed copy of Patrick's yearbook from the Boothbay Region High School. The entry mentioned that he starred in several theatrical productions and wanted to become an actor. He was in the drama and film club. On the electronic Yellow Pages, Joan was listed as a bookkeeper, a tax preparer, and a member of the Knox-Lincoln County Beekeepers.

That left Chip Granger. Alec had expected to see complaints about his workmanship on handyman websites. Instead, he found good reviews, which caused Alec to wonder whether they had been written by satisfied women and not their husbands.

It was twenty minutes past four when Alec closed his laptop and hurried downstairs, hoping the tea was still hot and there was plenty of babka left. Upon entering the parlor, Alec was greeted by Officer Taylor, Hillary, Paige, and Irena. The other guests were out sightseeing. Joan was taking a much-needed rest at her home after running the B&B by herself, and Patrick was at a rehearsal for his show.

Paige handed Alec a cup of English breakfast tea and a plate containing one large slice of cake. Winking, she said, "I saved this one for you. You're not the only person here who loves Karine's Cinnamon Babka."

Walt agreed. "It's very delicious. Hillary had to stop me from having a third portion. While you're here, tell me what happened when you saw Dr. Pierce at the hospital. I had planned to stop by but heard he's likely to be released this afternoon."

Alec settled back in the highbacked chair near the unlit fireplace and shook his head. "Alan told me that he didn't take the drugs by accident or on purpose. He believes they were stolen by someone who had no idea how dangerous it was to take an opioid with an anti-depressant or by someone who was aware of the risk and didn't care. Further, he thinks the medication had ended up in the wrong teacup and that no one had it in for him."

Walt reacted, "That's ridiculous! Either the man is very naïve, or he knows something."

"I looked up his credentials on the internet," Alec replied. "They were spotless. Could Leanne have mixed up the cups? She seemed shocked when her husband became ill."

Hillary spoke up then and said, "I've come to know Leanne pretty well and she's not the sort to take her own life or Alan's."

"No," Alec agreed. "Someone else may have tried to murder the good doctor yesterday and the poison was either administered at teatime or earlier in the day."

Officer Taylor sighed, "Leave it with me. I'll have a chat with Dr. Pierce tonight or tomorrow and find out what he and Leanne had for lunch on Sunday and where they dined. I suppose you washed out his teacup yesterday?"

Irena nodded. "I'm afraid Paige and I ran the dishwasher after teatime. We had no idea that anything was wrong until an hour later."

In response, Walt told them not to worry, and that he was going to call the hospital to confirm the results of Dr. Pierce's blood work. Rising from the couch, he added, "This evening, I plan to review everyone's police records. I didn't see anything noteworthy when Cassidy died but something may prove to be significant now."

Hillary saw her new beau to the door and returned to the others, asking if she could treat them to supper. Since Irena had no one to fill in for her, Hillary arranged for four lobster dinners to be delivered to the inn at seven o'clock.

Once the dirty dishes from teatime were placed in the dishwasher, Alec returned to the parlor where the women were comfortably settled. It wasn't long before their conversation turned to the blooming relationship between Hillary and the police chief. The decorator only admitted to enjoying his company, but her protestations said more.

Their topic then shifted to the subject of Maine, and Alec asked Irena about how she came to settle in Boothbay Harbor, so far from her three brothers and only sister. For the next two hours, Alec and Hillary learned a lot about Paige's rich family history.

Irena explained, "The first Andersons—Martin, his wife, Anna, and their son, Samuel, arrived in the USA from Rostock, Germany, in 1870. It was Samuel's son, Johann, who settled in Marshfield, Wisconsin. He, like his forefathers from the Baltic coast, was a dairy farmer."

Alec's question was not answered until Irena added, "My grandfather, Johann, married Vera Pavlova. She was born in Boothbay Harbor in 1892 and ran the family's boarding house before marrying grandad.

"That house stayed in the family, and Vera liked to bring me here as a child. Paige's father, my other brothers, and sister never showed much interest in visiting Boothbay Harbor. When Vera died in 1972, I inherited the inn."

Paige interjected, "My uncle Stefan has always been jealous and resents Aunt Irena for making such a success of Land's End."

Alec was beginning to formulate a picture of Paige's family dynamics and inquired, "So who was Great Grandpa, Yuri? Patrick told me that he sometimes haunts the third floor."

Hillary looked at Alec askance and Irena continued, "Yuri Pavlova was Vera's father and a whaler. He was born and raised in St. Petersburg, Russia, in 1848 and came to this country in 1878 when schooners began hunting humpbacks in the Gulf of Maine. A plant was set up in town to process whale oil and over the years, people moved to Boothbay.

"Yuri built the house in 1885. While he was at sea, my great grandmother Anna, Vera's mother, took in boarders to supplement their income. The foyer, parlor, and three of the rooms were part of the original building. Everything else came much later, and the older portions of the inn were slowly modernized."

Alec, still not sure how Yuri was related to Paige, asked Irena if she had a sketch of the family tree. Proudly, she removed a piece of paper from the sideboard and presented it to Alec.

It revealed Finnish and Russian Ancestry:

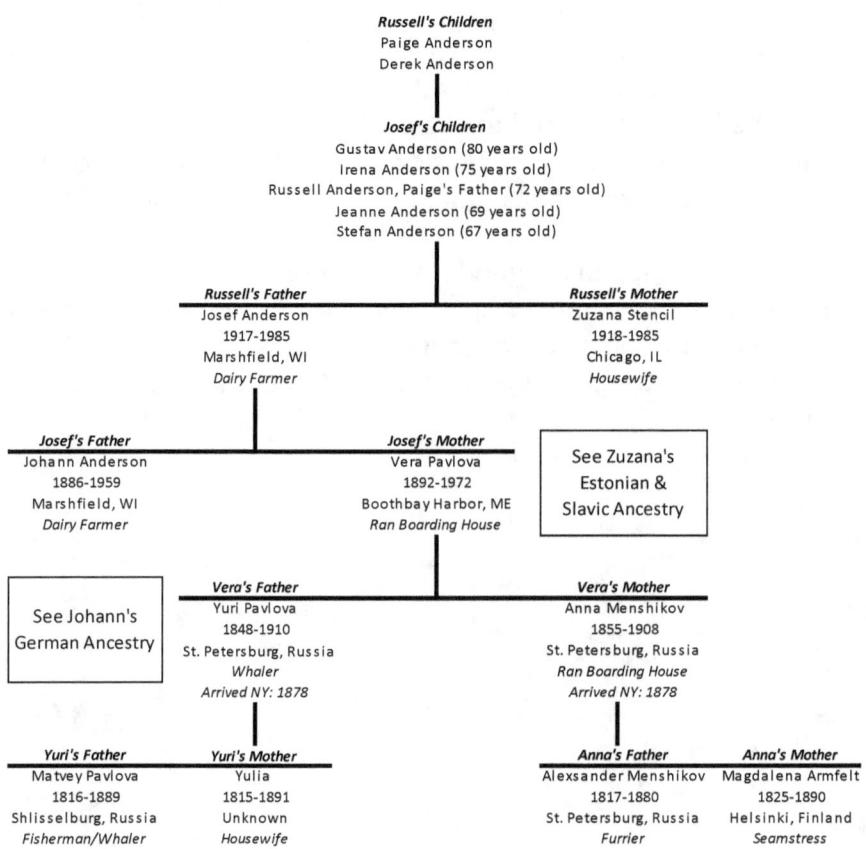

Russell's Children
Paige Anderson
Derek Anderson

Josef's Children
Gustav Anderson (80 years old)
Irena Anderson (75 years old)
Russell Anderson, Paige's Father (72 years old)
Jeanne Anderson (69 years old)
Stefan Anderson (67 years old)

Russell's Father		*Russell's Mother*
Josef Anderson		Zuzana Stencil
1917-1985		1918-1985
Marshfield, WI		Chicago, IL
Dairy Farmer		*Housewife*

Josef's Father	*Josef's Mother*	See Zuzana's
Johann Anderson	Vera Pavlova	Estonian &
1886-1959	1892-1972	Slavic Ancestry
Marshfield, WI	Boothbay Harbor, ME	
Dairy Farmer	*Ran Boarding House*	

See Johann's	*Vera's Father*	*Vera's Mother*
German Ancestry	Yuri Pavlova	Anna Menshikov
	1848-1910	1855-1908
	St. Petersburg, Russia	St. Petersburg, Russia
	Whaler	*Ran Boarding House*
	Arrived NY: 1878	*Arrived NY: 1878*

Yuri's Father	*Yuri's Mother*	*Anna's Father*	*Anna's Mother*
Matvey Pavlova	Yulia	Alexsander Menshikov	Magdalena Armfelt
1816-1889	1815-1891	1817-1880	1825-1890
Shlisselburg, Russia	Unknown	St. Petersburg, Russia	Helsinki, Finland
Fisherman/Whaler	*Housewife*	*Furrier*	*Seamstress*

Alec had new respect for the premises and what Irena had accomplished on her own. When he complemented her, she sighed, "I'm glad Joan will be able to take over. Running a B&B is for the young and energetic."

While the foursome was waiting for dinner to arrive, the Pierces returned to the inn from the hospital. Alan, appearing embarrassed, thanked Irena for extending their stay another two nights, promising to be out of her hair by Wednesday. Leanne then hurried her husband to their new room where Alan could rest and have a quiet evening.

After the Pierces ascended the stairway, Hillary asked Alec, "Have you two visited Bar Harbor yet? You really must go. It's about seventy miles north of Boothbay."

Excitedly, Paige turned to Alec, "I'd love to go!"

Irena seconded it and suggested for them to go the following morning since Joan was planning to fill in for a second day at the inn.

"Tomorrow sounds as good a day as any," Alec agreed. "Away from here, I may be able to figure out whether Judge Cassidy was murdered and who poisoned Alan Pierce."

A few minutes later, the food arrived, and everyone dug into their meal.

CHAPTER FIFTEEN

▼

"There Is a Mountain"
Words & Music by Donavan Leitch
Genre: Psychedelic Rock, Released: August 1967

Tuesday Morning—12th of July

Alec didn't waste a minute getting up and rushed Paige out of bed. After glimpsing at the time on her cellphone, she exclaimed, "It's 8:15 AM! I thought we were going to sleep in."

"Not this morning, Lass." Alec pronounced. "Bar Harbor may only be 70 miles north of here as the crow flies, but it's 116 miles by road. According to Google Maps, it's going to take about three hours to get to the tourist destination. First, we must head inland, then north, and eventually back to the coast."

Sitting up in bed, Paige frowned. "Do you still want to go? That's a lot of driving."

Alec smiled. "I'm really looking forward to the journey. I have a feeling it's going to be enlightening. Now, scoot into the shower. I'm going to run down to the kitchen and gather some food and drink for the car ride. Meet me downstairs. And don't forget to pack your camera and sweater. I hear it can be a bit cool on Cadillac Mountain."

Paige disappeared into the bathroom as Alec dressed for the outing.

Joan and Irena were preparing Tuesday's breakfast entrees when Alec greeted them. Hoping to get on the road by nine, Alec helped himself to a cup of hot coffee and asked, "Do you have a thermos or something similar?"

Irena indicated the place in the kitchen where she stored the insulated travel mugs. While Alec was filling up one for Paige, Irena asked, "What should I pack for you? I have leftover Banana Walnut Bread from yesterday and date nut from the day before."

"A few slices of each would be grand," Alec pronounced.

Joan was sautéing mushrooms and asparagus when she offered, "I can make you and Paige egg sandwiches for the road."

Although Alec was tempted to accept, he decided that the baked goods would carry them over till lunchtime. Upon arriving in Bar Harbor, he wanted to treat Paige to a hearty meal and then take her on the town's famous trolley to Acadia National Park.

Paige arrived minutes later and remarked, "I've managed to shower and dress in twenty minutes." Gratefully, she took the travel mug from Alec and the bag of goodies from her aunt. The twosome quickly said their goodbyes and took the kitchen's side door to Irena's car.

Alec plugged his cellphone's cord into the car's USB port and brought up the map and directions to Bar Harbor. From Land's End, the display showed that they would arrive at their destination by 11:32 AM. Alec started the car and said with panache, "Buckle up. We're about to go exploring."

Paige was too busy rummaging through the bag of snacks to react. After swallowing a piece of banana bread, she replied, "I'm glad the weather promises to be dry and sunny. A brochure I picked up at the inn says:

Acadia National Park is 76.7 square miles in size, and it's primarily located on Maine's Mount Desert Island off the coast of the Atlantic Ocean. Its landscape is marked by woodlands, rocky beaches, and glacier-scoured granite peaks. Cadillac Mountain is the highest point on the east coast of the United States. Among the wildlife are moose, bear, whales, and seabirds. The bayside town of Bar Harbor, with restaurants and shops, is a popular tourist gateway.

More invigorated than ever, Alec took Route 27 past familiar landmarks towards US-1 North. The road twisted and turned. At times, it looked like they were going in circles. Despite the circuitous route, Paige continually gazed at the map display on the car's monitor and advised Alec, "We're doing pretty well. I think we should arrive by eleven thirty."

The trip became more interesting as the car climbed up and down hills and headed north to Ellsworth. The couple realized they were on the final leg of their journey when the voice on Google Map instructed them to cross over Union River and take Route 3 East and South to Mount Desert Island.

Alec did not find the drive into Bar Harbor as scenic as the one into Boothbay Harbor. The road was more commercialized with large businesses and expensive hotels. The streets were crowded with cars and pedestrians. Alec had an especially hard time finding a parking spot near the center of town.

The pair eventually found metered parking at the Bar Harbor Club on West Street. After sitting so long in the car, Alec took a few moments to stretch his legs. He was glad that he and Paige had arrived early enough to have a nice lunch before going on the four-star trolley ride to Acadia National Park at 1:00 PM.

Once they collected their belongings, the twosome locked the car and headed toward Oli's Trolley to collect the tickets that Alec had purchased online. When they were safely tucked away in his wallet, Alec directed Paige further down West Street where they could have an early lunch at Stewman's Downtown Lobster Pound.

The couple asked for seating outside on the pier where they could enjoy the sunshine and fresh air. Alec was hungry and ordered a fried seafood platter. Paige, on the other hand, had nibbled on too many baked goods in the car and chose a burger with sweet potato fries. Alec felt sure he could polish off Paige's meal if she was unable to finish hers.

Despite their close proximity to Oli's Trolly Depot, Alec and Paige had to be mindful of the time. Alec was pleased with their lunch and the restaurant's ambiance. When he realized it was nearing one o'clock, he quickly paid the tab and hurried Paige out of the eatery. Tickets for the two excursions had cost one hundred and fifty dollars, and Alec did not want to miss the tour.

Luckily, there were other stragglers, and the tour guide made it a point to match up the ticket holders with the number of passengers seated in the trolley. Alec and Paige found comfortable seats on the right side of the vehicle. The guide, Jim, looked like a former military man and spoke with great authority, explaining that he was retired and a longtime resident of Bar Harbor.

When his numbers tallied, Jim asked everyone to silence their cell phones and took a seat behind the wheel. As he maneuvered the trolley past Jackson Laboratory, a famous research institute, and then south on Park Loop Road, Jim told his passengers about the Great Fire of 1947 that had spread over 17,188 acres of the park. When the fire encompassed the roads leading in and out of Bar Harbor, many of the townspeople were forced to escape the flames by sea.

The trolley entered the park at the Sieur de Monts entrance where Jim paid the admission fee. After driving a few minutes, he pointed out Sand Beach, which was nestled in a small inlet between the granite mountains and the rocky shores of Mount Desert Island.

The beach was 290 yards long and its sand contained unique fragments of seashells, which had been crushed by the pounding surf. Alec wasn't able to catch anyone in the water and when Jim announced that the water rarely exceeded 55 degrees, Alec understood why.

A half mile from Sand Beach was Thunder Hole. It was named that because of the loud roar the waves made while crashing into a small cavern beneath the surface of the water. The noise sounded like distant thunder and at times those waves splashed forty feet into the air.

Just past Thunder Hole, Jim stopped the trolley for his passengers to stretch their legs and admire the park's beauty up close. Alec and Paige were glad to get out and walk along the ocean path that ran parallel to the road. To their left were massive rock formations that jutted into the blue sea. Many of their fellow sightseers hiked onto the slippery stones while others were content to sit on slabs of granite and watch nature work from a distance.

Alec was bolder than Paige and coaxed her to move closer to the edge of the rugged cliffs. She had to admit, the view was worth the climb.

Once back in the trolley, Jim explained, "The mountain peaks in Acadia National Park are part of the Appalachian Mountain Range. The Appalachian's run two thousand miles from Northern Alabama to the island of Newfoundland in Canada. Most of the U.S. mountain range is a considerable distance from the Atlantic Ocean. Here in Maine, visitors to Bar Harbor can see these magnificent mountains touch the sea."

Jim's statement took on more significance as the trolley rounded Otter Point and Alec spied the mountains that seemed to appear and disappear as the vehicle traveled along Park Loop Road. Despite the people sitting near him, Alec sang out,

> The lock upon my garden gate's a snail, that's what it is
> The lock upon my garden gate's a snail, that's what it is
> First there is a mountain, then there is no mountain, then there is
> First there is a mountain, then there is no mountain, then there is
>
> The caterpillar sheds his skin to find a butterfly within

Caterpillar sheds his skin to find a butterfly within
First there is a mountain, then there is no mountain, then there is
First there is a mountain, then there is no mountain

Oh Juanita, oh Juanita, oh Juanita, I call your name
Oh, the snow will be a blinding sight to see as it lies on yonder hillside

The lock upon my garden gate's a snail, that's what it is
The lock upon my garden gate's a snail, that's what it is
Caterpillar sheds his skin to find a butterfly within
Caterpillar sheds his skin to find a butterfly within

First there is a mountain, then there is no mountain, then there is
First there is a mountain, then there is no mountain, then there is
First there is a mountain, then there is no mountain, then there is
First there is a mountain, then there is no mountain, then there is
First there is a mountain

Paige tried to get Alec to lower his voice but was unable to accomplish the deed. Instead, she turned to the people sitting behind them and muttered, "He's Scottish," hoping it explained his behavior.

Alec merely laughed, "I'll have you know that song was written by one of my countrymen. And it definitely fits in with our current landscape."

"I think," Paige whispered, "Donovan must have been stoned when he wrote those lyrics. What do mountains have to do with a snail that resembles a lock on a garden gate?"

Alec argued, "His song had to do with change, Lass. Nothing ever stays the same. Caterpillars become butterflies, new peaks erupt from the ocean floor, and mountain tops erode."

Their conversation was cut short when the guide announced, "Our next stop is going to be Jordan Pond House and Restaurant where you can buy souvenirs, have some refreshments, and view the area from the building's second story balcony. Also, be sure to take photographs of the house's lovely gardens."

While a few sightseers hurried to the bathrooms and store, Alec and Paige mounted the steps to the lookout. There was a sign telling them that the property was donated to the park by John D. Rockefeller Jr. in 1940. Another display explained that the pond in front of them was formed by a mile-thick glacier. As the glacier melted in the valley, it left behind a mound of rock, gravel, and sand called a moraine that became Jordan Pond.

After perusing the shop, Paige and Alec left empty handed hoping they could purchase less expensive items in the town of Bar Harbor. When everyone was back on the trolley, Jim advised that their final stop was going to be Cadillac Mountain, Acadia's highest peak on the east coast of the U.S. at 1,530 feet.

The trolley pulled into its designated parking spot once it was able to maneuver around improperly parked cars and buses in a holding pattern. There were lots of people around them, all making their way along a half-mile-long path to the peak's summit. Alec and Paige followed behind the other sightseers.

The view from the mountain top was breathtaking. After gazing at the ocean dotted with barren islands, Alec stopped to take a picture of a poster entitled, "Islands Galore," It showed all the land masses that could be seen from their vantage point.

He and Paige were able to make out some of them as he read, "Two million, five hundred thousand people visit this park every year. And Mount Desert Island is Maine's largest island at 108 square miles. I had no idea."

The poster also showed the couple how Cadillac Mountain looked during each season. Although it remained quite desolate with little foliage during all four seasons, you could see how spring varied from fall and summer from winter.

Despite the sunny weather, Paige began to feel chilled and put on a sweater she had stuffed inside her tote bag. Together, the pair explored the summit and walked close to overhanging rock ledges to view the crystal blue waters below.

Alec had to check his watch to make sure they weren't going to be tardy on their return to the trolley. Once everyone was aboard, Jim made a final count and started up the vehicle. He invited everyone to return to Acadia National Park again and to visit the town, recommending a few places to eat and shop. Paige eagerly asked where she could purchase park souvenirs, and he named several stores on Main Street.

The trip back to the trolley depot took no time at all. After disembarking, Alec and Paige set off for the primary shopping area. Their first stop was a store that sold wild Maine blueberry jam and a six-inch sachet containing pieces of balsam pinecones. The pouch was less expensive than those they saw at the Jordan Pond shop, and they smelled just as fragrant. Mindful that they were going on a European cruise after leaving Maine, Paige was unable to buy everything she wanted.

While walking along the busy street with their purchases, Alec suggested ice cream. Jim had remarked that Mainers or "Mainiacs" ingested more ice cream per year than citizens of any other state. Even though his comment didn't sound entirely true to Alec, he was all for trying one of the town's homemade treats.

At a nearby shop, Alec ordered two scoops of banana chocolate chunk ice cream for himself and Maine blueberry soft serve for Paige. While the couple was watching Paige's creamy blue ice cream pass through the machine's metal chute and tumble into the waffle cone, Alec called out, "I know who murdered Richard Cassidy! His killer nearly got away with it by making the judge's death appear to be an accident."

The fellow behind the counter eyed Alec with suspicion and asked if he wanted anything else. After paying for their ice cream, Paige rushed Alec out of the store and made him sit on a bench along Main Street. Before tasting her blueberry frozen dessert, Paige demanded, "Who did it? And, what about Alan Pierce? Did someone try to kill him or was it less sinister?"

While they enjoyed their snack on a sunny bench, Alec shared his suspicions. Together, they came up with a plan to amass some proof. Exuberantly, the twosome returned to their car and took the long trip back to Boothbay Harbor.

It was nearly 8:00 o'clock when the DunBartons returned to the bed and breakfast. Irena must have heard them come in and emerged from her room, wearing a bathrobe and pushing her walker. She welcomed them in her customarily warm manner before searching Paige's face. She then exclaimed, "You know, don't you?"

The trio made themselves comfortable in the breakfast room. While Paige was placing a sandwich in front of her husband, Alec expounded upon his theory.

Irena listened carefully and then suggested, "You'd better speak to Chief Taylor tonight. I understand he's at home right now. Hillary is planning to stay at his house after she checks out of the inn on Thursday, and he's apparently getting his 'bachelor pad' ready for her."

Alec laughed and had Paige sit down to eat. When they polished off their sandwiches and ended their meal with leftover scones, Alec called the officer. Although Alec offered to meet him, Walt agreed to stop by the inn in thirty minutes.

Police Chief Taylor arrived a short time later. The ladies excused themselves—Paige to take a hot bath and Irena to watch TV in her room.

While the men were sipping whisky, Alec asked the officer, "Can you get me a complete list of Cassidy's judicial cases while he was a judge and a district attorney? You may have to go all the way back to when Cassidy first joined the bar. I know *who* killed Cassidy but not *why*. I believe the reason lies in the judge's past."

Walt grunted, "My officers had gone through the records, but they could have missed something. I'll get the cases over to you first thing in the morning. In the meantime, what do you need regarding physical proof?"

Alec lowered his voice and began, "First, I want you to get a search warrant for one particular item in the inn. I'd also like to invite everyone who was present at the July 4th fireworks to be here by 11:00 AM tomorrow. We can assemble in the breakfast room. I'll make sure to include Paige, Irena, Joan, Patrick, Karine, the Pierces and Hillary." Alec watched Taylor's expression as he uttered Hillary's name but saw no emotion on his face.

Taylor agreed and added, "I'll get one of my officers to bring Chip Granger in. Do you think two armed individuals will be able to handle the arrest?"

Alec nodded his head in the affirmative, "I doubt you'll require anyone else. You should have no problem bringing in Cassidy's killer."

CHAPTER SIXTEEN

▼

"Don't Let Me Be Misunderstood"
Words & Music by Bennie Benjamin,
Horace Ott, and Sol Marcus
Genre: Blues Rock, Released: February 1965

Wednesday Morning—13th of July

Alec had a sleepless night wondering what drove Cassidy's killer to commit the crime. He was sure it had to do with how Richard conducted himself as a judge in Lincoln County or as a district attorney in Cumberland County. Cassidy was a narcissistic man, only out for himself regardless of how his decisions affected others.

When Paige awoke at 2:00 AM to use the bathroom, she found her husband staring at the ceiling and asked, "Is there anything I can do to help you fall asleep?"

Alec winked in response and Paige scolded, "That isn't what I had in mind."

Instead, she offered, "Why don't you share your thoughts. Are you worried you've picked the wrong culprit?"

Alec propped up his pillow and made room for Paige to sit beside him. As he enumerated the reasons why he felt certain he had the right person, Alec's eyes grew tired, and his head sank back down on the pillow.

The alarm clock woke them both at seven o'clock. Alec jumped out of bed with renewed energy, despite having less than five hours of sleep. He was able to shave, shower, and dress within fifteen minutes.

Paige, afraid that Alec would rush her unnecessarily, told him to go down to the kitchen without her. Alec did not need to be coaxed and kissed his wife's cheeks as she was about to bathe.

From their suite on the third floor, Alec strode down the inside staircase. He found Chief Taylor sitting in the parlor with manila-colored folders on his lap and spread all over the sofa.

Upon seeing Alec, he remarked, "I'm glad you didn't sleep in this morning. I went through the judge's files and found a few cases in which Cassidy showed bias towards influential people in his circle."

Just as Alec was about to take a seat next to the officer, Irena popped out of the kitchen to offer the men freshly brewed coffee and to let Alec know that she would be able to handle most of the food preparation and cooking herself.

With nothing hampering him now, Alec dove into the files. Several of the findings that Cassidy came up with while serving on the bench appeared questionable. Though his verdicts may have been unsound, Alec found himself more interested in the names of victims and complainants whose crimes never made it to court.

Alec pointed to the name of one plaintive and asked Walt, "Why wouldn't a district attorney try this case in court?"

After glancing at the list, Taylor quickly wrote down the docket number and replied, "District Attorneys don't like to take cases they can't win. In this case, however, there may have been a nefarious reason. If I can't pull the file from the court's internet, I'll retrieve a copy from Cumberland Courthouse and get it to you by ten, at the latest."

As Walt was rising from the couch, Paige appeared in the parlor and asked, "Did you find what you needed?"

Alec escorted the chief to the inn's front door and responded, "I think we're going to be in good shape."

Alec and Paige were able to help Irena prepare the remaining breakfast entrees. The couple that checked in on Monday afternoon consumed a Ham and Cheese Parcel before going on a whale watching excursion.

The only other guest staying at the inn was a woman from Jacksonville, Florida. She had come north to visit her daughter's family in nearby Edgecomb, Maine. She departed to babysit her two grandsons soon after finishing a stack of blueberry pancakes.

The Pierces came down for breakfast at 9:00 o'clock, hungry and talkative. Since they planned to visit their eldest son in Portsmouth, New Hampshire, before returning home to Vermont, they were in no rush to checkout. Their son's home was only a two hours' drive from Boothbay Harbor.

Hillary was steps behind the Pierces, and Leanne made room for her at their breakfast table. Over the past ten days, Hillary had become good friends with Leanne. They shared an interest in antiques and home decorating. The two women even made plans to get together in Manhattan, where the Pierce's youngest son had a small apartment.

Alan opted for the ham and cheese dish and the ladies were content to have coffee and Pumpkin Cranberry Bread, expressing hope that they hadn't gained too much weight while staying at Land's End. Concerned that they might not stay in the immediate vicinity, Alec asked, "Would you mind returning to the breakfast room at eleven. I believe Irena wants to say or give you something before you go."

All three of them looked pleased. Alec didn't have to be as diplomatic with Patrick and Karine. Both arrived at ten and didn't mind that their workday was going to be delayed an hour. That left only Joan Bishop. Despite having her hand's full the day before, Joan said she would stop by the inn at eleven.

While the Pierces were packing up their trunk with last minute items, Hillary excused herself to freshen up. Eager to hear from Walt, Alec waited near the inn's reception area, looking for his car to pull up. The police chief arrived minutes later and handed Alec a thin file, remarking, "I think you'll find it very interesting."

Alec was scanning the information when Paige and Irena announced that the breakfast room was tidy. Karine and Patrick were the first to take seats in the room after helping themselves to leftover food in the kitchen. The Pierces came in next and were followed by Hillary and Joan.

Chip Granger was the last to arrive accompanied by one of Taylor's officers. The handyman didn't seem too annoyed by the policeman's request and took his seat with the others.

When everyone was settled, Alec stood up in the room and announced, "Before we go our separate ways today, I wanted to say goodbye to the Pierces and to also address Cassidy's death. You may have noticed that the room is now filled with everyone who had witnessed the judge's *accident* on July 4th

"I have permission from Officer Taylor to tell you what I think happened to Richard Cassidy and about the attempt that was made on Dr. Pierce's life. I hope none of you will mind."

Alec looked at the faces of those assembled. None of them appeared to be alarmed. Walt nodded for him to continue, and Alec pronounced, "I'm quite sure that the judge was murdered in plain sight of nine witnesses during the fireworks display."

Hillary spoke up first and said, "Cassidy was stung by a bee. How could anyone get an insect to do that on purpose."

Alec agreed, "You can't, not even Joan Bishop, our mistress of the bees, could accomplish that.

"No," Alec resumed, "Judge Cassidy was *not* stung by a bee! A person near him injected a hypodermic needle full of bee venom into his right buttock. At the same time, a dead bee was dropped onto the floor of the balcony to make it appear that he was stung. I found the insect after the judge was taken to the hospital and gave it to Officer Taylor later that night.

"The question is, 'How was the bee venom collected?'"

Joan piped up. "It's easy to collect bee venom. An electrically charged device with a glass shield needs to be placed near the hive. When the electricity is turned on, the bees sting the glass without harm to them. Afterward, an apiarist can scrape off the venom. The dry venom looks like white crystals and can be reconstituted later into various medications and skin-care products."

Alec nodded and posed to Joan, "Can you collect honeybee venom in an ordinary glass jar?"

"Yes," Joan replied, "It wouldn't be too difficult to scoop the bees up while they're swarming around their hive and flowers. Anyone trying to catch them that way would no doubt get stung."

As an afterthought, Joan added, "Bees will die quickly if left in a glass jar and exposed to strong sunlight and hot temperatures."

Alec thanked Joan for the information and hypothesized aloud, "The killer could have collected the venom in a glass jar, mixed it with some saline, and injected it into Cassidy. Now, I need to ask who and why?"

Dr. Pierce stirred in his seat and stated forcefully, "I tried to save him, not once, but twice. I followed the correct protocol and administered the epinephrine at the right times. You were all there!"

Alec acknowledged his statement and replied, "That's why I never suspected you. The police lab concluded that the contents of the EpiPen contained exactly what it was supposed to. You did everything humanly possible to keep Cassidy alive. It was not until this morning that Walt and I found a motive for you to murder him."

Leanne cried out, "You're crazy! Alan wouldn't hurt a fly. This room is filled with people who hated the judge."

"That's true," Alec agreed. "Both Patrick and Joan have or will profit monetarily from Cassidy's death. Karine's husband had a run-in with the judge over his lobster business, and Chip Granger was being sued by the man. Hillary Fairchild was stalked by Richard and made to fear for her life. Even Paige's sweet aunt was glad to see the end of him and will eventually profit by his death. Everyone despised Richard Cassidy, everyone but the Pierces."

"That's no reason to suspect us," Alan complained. "We hardly knew him. This is pointless. Come on, Leanne, we're leaving! They have absolutely no proof I did anything wrong."

From a chair in the corner of the room, Walt ordered them to stay put. At the same time, he reached for a black medical bag that was under his seat and held it up.

To Alec, the police chief announced, "You were correct. A one milliliter syringe was missing from Dr. Pierce's list of medical supplies. We found it in his discarded sharps container, and I believe it contains rehydrated bee venom."

Now standing, Taylor addressed Alan Pierce and asked, "Why didn't you dispose of the murder weapon somewhere else? Without it, we wouldn't have had enough to charge you!"

At that point, Alan cried out like a trapped animal. Leanne looked at her husband in horror and screamed, "Why did you kill him? You promised to do no harm in your Hippocratic Oath!"

The officer who had brought in Chip Granger moved closer to Dr. Pierce and had him stand up, quoting,

You have the right to remain silent. Anything you say can and will be used against you in a court of law. You have the right to an attorney. If you cannot afford an attorney, one will be provided for you. Do you understand the rights I have just read to you? With these rights in mind, do you wish to speak to me?

Alan looked around the room, appearing to have calmed down. Speaking clearly, the doctor said, "I want to make a statement here and now. You need to know what that despicable man did to me and my family!"

Walt quickly turned on his phone's tape recorder and nodded for him to go on. Retaking his seat, Alan explained, "Eighteen years ago, our only daughter attended the University of New England in Portland. She was majoring in the health sciences and wanted to do something to help people. She was beautiful and had a sweet soul."

The doctor's voice cracked, and Leanne put her arm around her husband's shoulder as he continued, "On the night before she was due to come home for Christmas break, she was hit by a car at the crosswalk of a busy street and died at the scene from multiple injuries. I may have been able to accept that if it hadn't been for other factors.

"The driver ran a red light. The police gave him a breathalyzer test and learned that his blood alcohol concentration was just under the limit for Maine drivers. They also found he had been taking meclizine for vertigo. The combination of the two drugs had most certainly reduced his ability to remain mentally alert."

Alec found himself getting angry. His first wife and daughter had been killed by a drunk driver, and he still experienced pain that would well up unexpectantly and then disappear just as quickly.

Alan sighed, "The worst part of it was the way the District Attorney's Office handled the case. Richard Cassidy was in charge and had concluded that the 'evidence, while horrible and tragic, did not rise to the level of criminal culpability.'

"The driver, who belonged to the same country club as Richard Cassidy, was found to be going 39 mph in a 35-mph speed limit zone. Even though he was over the posted speed limit, an engineer with the Department of Transportation said that 40 mph was the proper speed for the area.

"Cassidy determined that his 'good friend' had hit the gas instead of the brake because of a severe medical event. What hogwash! That man was negligent and should have been charged with vehicular manslaughter for driving while taking meclizine with alcohol."

Irena shook her head in sadness and Hillary remarked, "Dick was a vile man. Did you later sue the driver in a civil suit?"

Leanne replied, "The driver died a year after the car accident occurred from cancer, and I convinced Alan to let it go. I was very depressed at the time and attending Compassionate Friends to deal with my bereavement."

Alan snickered, "That bastard didn't even recognize me when Irena introduced us at the inn. I must have been to Cassidy's office a half dozen times. I didn't say anything to him, deciding to be the better man and let bygones be bygones.

"I even tried to save him when he ingested the honey spice cake. What a fool I was. Richard Cassidy deserved to die by my hand or should I say a bee's stinger. Upon learning how allergic he was to bee venom, I gave him a large enough injection to kill him within minutes. I'm actually surprised he lasted so long."

The police officer was about to lead the doctor away when Alec held up his hand and asked, "If you were so sure you did the right thing, why did you try to kill yourself a few days later?"

Alan crumpled into the arms of the officer and confessed, "Murder is never acceptable. I needed to pay for what I did."

After Alan was led away by Chief Taylor and his fellow officer, Leanne turned to Hillary and burst into tears. Irena hurried over to the kitchen with her walker and returned with a large glass of brandy. Leanne didn't need any coaxing to drink it and then began to cough when she swallowed too much at one time. Paige was in the thick of things trying to help.

Patrick seemed the most relieved and heartily thanked Alec. Joan was equally happy to hear that she and her son were no longer suspects in Cassidy's death. Shortly later, they departed, Patrick to his post at the front desk and Joan to attend to her bees.

Karine stopped by long enough to give Alec a kiss on the cheek before starting her housekeeping chores. Chip Granger was the last to leave, commenting, "I never thought of killing him, but I'm glad someone did."

The four women remained in the breakfast room until Leanne was calm enough to call her sons and a lawyer for Alan. Anxious to get away from the scene of the crime and Alec, the man who proved that Cassidy's death was not an accident, Leanne gathered up her belongings to leave.

Not sure she was capable of driving, Alec watched Mrs. Pierce depart and felt a deep sense of sympathy as she drove away. Thinking about Alan and how Leanne reacted, Alec sang out,

Baby, do you understand me now
Sometimes I feel a little mad
Well, don't you know that no-one alive
Can always be an angel
When things go wrong. I seem to be bad

I'm just a soul whose intentions are good
Oh Lord, please don't let me be misunderstood
If I seem edgy, I want you to know
That I never meant to take it out on you
Life has its problems and I've got my share
And that's one thing I never meant to do

'Cause I love you
Baby, don't you know I'm just human
And I've thoughts like any other man
And sometimes I find myself alone and regretting
Some foolish thing, some foolish thing I've done

But I'm just a soul whose intentions are good
Oh Lord, please don't let me be misunderstood

If I seem edgy, I want you to know
That I never meant to take it out on you
Life has its problems and I've got my share
And that's one thing I never meant to do

'Cause I love you
Baby, don't you know I'm just human
And I've thoughts like any other man
But sometimes I find myself alone regretting
Some foolish thing, some foolish thing I've done

But I'm just a soul whose intentions are good
Oh Lord, please don't let me be misunderstood

'Cause I'm just a soul whose intentions are good
Oh Lord, please don't let me be misunderstood

Oh Lord, don't let me be misunderstood
Don't let me be, don't let me be misunderstood

After uttering the last verse, Alec was joined by Hillary and Paige. Despite feeling bad for Leanne, Hillary remarked, "I'm glad it's all settled. Walt felt very uncomfortable with the situation, especially since we're seeing each other. He knew I had nothing to do with Richard's death, but now everyone else knows."

Paige agreed and the two women decided the only way to dispel their sense of gloom was to go shopping.

CHAPTER SEVENTEEN

"Secret O' Life"
Words & Music by James Taylor
Genre: Folk Rock, Released: June 1977

Wednesday Evening—13th of July

At 6:00 PM, Alec moved the barbecue from the side of the inn to the first-floor balcony. The charcoals were just beginning to turn grey and approaching the correct temperature. In the breakfast room, Alec had six well-seasoned and thick ribeye steaks sitting on a table along with a pile of husked corn.

Alec could hear Paige in the kitchen with her aunt making a huge salad and discussing which salad dressing to take out of the refrigerator. Alec ducked into the room long enough to remind them to make some lemonade while grabbing a six pack of chilled beer.

The DunBartons and Irena had everything ready by the time Officer Taylor and his date, Hillary Fairchild, arrived for the celebratory dinner at six-thirty. Besides beer and lemonade, the company was invited to have mixed drinks. To make it even more festive, Irena put out her famous spinach dip and buttery mini quiches, which contained cheese and mushrooms.

After everyone was settled on the balcony deck with appetizers and drinks, Alec got to his feet and toasted, "To Paige who wanted soft serve blueberry ice cream in Bar Harbor. To Irena, who gave me insights into suicide, and to Walt, who allowed me to amass all my suspects in one room like a detective on a television series."

Before anyone could take a drink, Hillary snapped, "What about me? I'm not just a pretty face."

Alec winked at her and quickly added, "To Hillary, for making Officer Taylor happy and for not being a killer."

Hillary laughed and they all agreed it was a time to celebrate.

While Paige was passing around the hors d'oeurves, Irena asked, "I want to know how Paige's choice of ice cream helped you solve the case. And why couldn't you accept that Cassidy's death was an accident? Boothbay is always filled with bees in July and August and it's not unusual for people to get stung."

Hillary muttered, "I'm not surprised he was murdered. He alienated everyone—his own family, so-called friends, fellow workers, and the townspeople."

Paige agreed with Hillary and Alec remarked, "I had no reason to think Cassidy was cold-bloodedly killed. As Irena mentioned, there are bees all over the place and Joan has a hive just over the hedge.

"It was obvious that Richard was highly allergic to bee venom after having a severe reaction to the honey in Irena's spice cake. A dead bee, minus its stinger, was found on the porch. It all seemed plausible. No," Alec conceded, "I suspected a crime because I have a suspicious nature."

Walt laughed. "I must have a suspicious nature too. Even though I wanted to believe he had a stroke of bad luck, I couldn't let it go either."

Gazing at Hillary, Walt admitted, "You were my first suspect."

Alec agreed, "Cassidy threatened Hillary's safety and security when he electronically stalked her. I can't imagine how you felt when you learned he was staying at the same inn that you booked months earlier."

Paige visibly shivered. "I thought Joan made a likely suspect. Mothers can be very protective of their children, and Cassidy was such a horrid man. Joan had probably been relieved when Richard gave her child support in one lump sum. That way she never had to set eyes on him again or wait for his support check."

Hillary nodded. "I was afraid that Patrick did it. He gained the most financially. Now, he's able to afford college and help his mother buy the inn. His father despised his career choice and had no interest in him."

Irena was pretty quiet up till then but admitted, "I was worried that Karine had something to do with Cassidy's death. She's an extremely loyal person and would do anything to shield me and her husband from harm. She had plenty of reason to hate the judge."

"Isn't it interesting that no one suspected Chip or the Pierces?" Alec remarked. "I didn't think Chip was intelligent enough to make a murder look like an accident, and the Pierces had no discernable reason to dislike him. I'm also certain that Alan did everything he could do to save Cassidy the first time."

Finishing his drink, Walt concurred. "The EpiPens contained the right dosage of medicine and were administered at the proper times. Officials at the lab and the hospital confirmed that the doctor followed the correct protocols."

Paige refilled the glasses while Alec placed the steaks and corn on the charcoal grill. Although Irena still had to depend upon a walker to get around, she was able to bring out a surprising number of items from the kitchen. In minutes, the outside patio table was filled with salad, condiments, and seasonings.

Little was discussed when their meal was ready. The fivesome was happy to enjoy the food, the setting sun, and the gentle breezes off the inner harbor. Alec and Walt shared the last ribeye steak, and Paige and Hillary complemented Irena on her delicious salad.

While Paige cleared the table, Walt asked Alec, "What made you first suspect Alan Pierce of Cassidy's murder?"

Alec made himself comfortable on the outdoor cushioned chair with his scotch and replied. "It was shortly after Cassidy died. Before then, Alan was a rather reserved individual and showed little emotion. Afterward he showed more animation and behaved as though he had made up his mind to do something.

"Later, when Dr, Pierce was hospitalized and we went through his medical bag, I heard the rattle of an object in the sharps container but gave it no thought.

"It was also clear that Alan was a methodical man and took his Hippocratic Oath seriously. He not only kept an up-to-date list of his equipment and medications in his doctor's bag but also had probably placed the venom filled syringe in the sharps container to prevent an innocent person from getting pricked by it.

"When Irena mentioned that suicide was a person's way to escape pain, fear, or emptiness, I realized that Alan could have tried to kill himself. He may have hated himself for taking revenge upon a flawed human being. It might have been his way to make amends and keep Leanne from finding out that her husband was not the man she thought he was."

Paige, who had just joined the others, interrupted, "When Alec shared his suspicions with me, I wondered why Alan had purposely overdosed while staying here. Now, I think he was trying to protect Leanne. Back in Vermont, she would have been alone and devastated to find her husband dead. Here, she had friends and people who could help her deal with it all."

Irena murmured, "I feel like most of my guests *are* family."

Hillary smiled, "I'm glad you count me as one, But, getting back to the murder, what did Paige's ice cream choice have to do with solving the murder?"

After taking a mouthful of his whisky, Alec answered, "It was the way the soft serve came out of the ice cream machine's metal nozzle. It reminded me of fluid being pushed through a syringe. Once I figure out how the bee venom was administered, it left me to wonder who and why.

"We were all present when Cassidy died, but only one person was actually stung on the hand that morning. That person was Alan Pierce. He probably received the sting while rounding up the bees for their venom. I also couldn't see anyone else in our circle expertly injecting the poison into the judge's butt.

"The 'why' was rather easy to figure out. Walt found an old case, which Cassidy oversaw while he was serving as district attorney in Portland. A young woman, Anna Pierce, was killed in a vehicular accident by an associate of Cassidy's. It must have broken the Pierces' hearts when the case was not tried in court and even more of a shock when Alan learned that the person responsible for the miscarriage of justice was staying at Land's End!"

Irena found herself getting angry and declared, "I'm not sorry he's dead. I just wish that Alan Pierce hadn't done it. What's going to happen to him?"

It was Walt's turn to chime in and he replied, "The district attorney in Lincoln County was given the case this afternoon. Leanne and her sons have hired a well-known law firm. His legal team has agreed to let Dr. Pierce 'plead guilty' for a reduced sentence. The court may go easy on him, and the doctor voiced a desire to use his medical skills in prison to help his fellow inmates. I think it will turn out okay for him and Leanne."

For the remainder of the evening, the dinner guests discussed their plans for the rest of the summer. Hillary knew she would have to return to her office in New York sooner than later but promised to be back in the fall to see the leaves change. Smiling up at her beau, Hillary added, it will be wonderful to cuddle up with Walt by a fire in his cabin."

Walt expressed his thanks to Alec for wrapping up the murder case in ten days and was eager to investigate simple robberies and assaults again. Winking at the others, he stated. "I also plan to go to New York City, my old stomping ground, at the end of the summer. I have two weeks of vacation coming and a lovely woman to visit."

Irena sighed and sweetly acknowledged, "I have everything a person could want. I know Joan will be able to care for my former guests, and I'll be able to help her during the hectic summer months. Patrick, the darling boy, will have an opportunity to go to acting school, and Karine will continue to have a job she loves with a substantial pay raise.

"Best of all, I have a terrific niece and handsome nephew who have solved a confusing murder, are helping me run my B&B, and will be escorting me to Denmark in three weeks' time for the cruise of a lifetime."

Thinking about what it takes to have a peaceful life, Alec crooned,

> The secret of life is enjoying the passage of time
> Any fool can do it
> There ain't nothing to it
> Nobody knows how we got to the top of the hill
> But since we're on our way down
> We might as well enjoy the ride
>
> The secret of love is in opening up your heart
> It's okay to feel afraid
> But don't let that stand in your way
> 'Cause anyone knows that love is the only road
> And since we're only here for a while
> We might as well show some style
>
> Give us a smile
> Isn't it a lovely ride?
> Sliding down, gliding down
> Try not to try too hard
> It's a lovely ride
> Isn't it a lovely ride?
> Sliding down, I'll be gliding down
> Try not to try too hard
> It's just a lovely ride
>
> Now the secret of life is enjoying the passage of time
> Any fool can do it
> Ain't nothing to it
> Nobody knows how we got to the top of the hill
> But since we're on our way down
> We might as well enjoy the ride

Hillary applauded when Alec finished the song and confirmed, "You, or should I say, James Taylor, is so right. I've learned during the past few days to savor my life and the friendships I've made. Work is secondary and people need to enjoy the passage of time even when things get tough. New adventures can be around the corner."

Walt smiled and announced, "It's time for us to say goodnight. Hillary will return tomorrow to pack up her belongings and officially check out, and I'll keep you posted on how Alan and Leanne are doing."

With that said, Alec, Paige, and Irena escorted the couple to the door. Eager for bed, Irena excused herself, and the DunBartons quickly cleaned the kitchen and hurried off to their suite. While Alec was having a quick smoke on the third-floor deck, he watched Paige prepare and undress for her evening bath.

When she disappeared into the bathroom, he set his pipe down and followed her, just in time to see his wife submerge her naked body under glistening warm bubbles.

Life was back to normal, and Alec was going to enjoy the next three weeks with his family and new friends.

EPILOGUE

—————————▼—————————

**Friday Morning
5th of August
9:05 AM EDT**

Alec and Paige had just finished packing up the trunk of Irena's car, when Patrick called from the inn's foyer, "Are you about ready? Irena is worried that we're going to miss the plane to New York."

Alec glanced at his watch, and it read 9:05 AM. "We've got everything in. I'm afraid Irena and Paige are going to be a bit cramped in the backseat. All together, we have six pieces of luggage and two carryon bags."

"Make that three." Irena called as she surefootedly approached the car. "I've packed a few goodies for the first leg of our journey. The food on the plane to JFK can't really be called food, and I know Alec will probably need a snack even before we leave the ground at Portland International Jetport."

As Paige helped her aunt into the backseat, Joan Bishop approached the car to give Irena a kiss and warn, "I don't want you to worry about anything while you're gone. After Patrick gets back from the airport, he's going to confirm the remaining reservations for the month and send out thank you notes to past visitors. Karine is going to start the heavy cleaning, and Chip is coming by later to spruce up the garden."

Irena sighed, "You're such a dear. I don't know what I would have done without you. It's a comfort to know that the inn is in such good hands."

Patrick, wearing the same chauffeur's cap he had on the day he picked up the DunBartons, ordered Alec and Paige into the car and got behind the wheel. Alec had to adjust his front seat to make more leg room, forcing Paige, who was behind him, to move her knees sideways.

Paige, expressing relief that the trip to the airport was only going to take an hour and a quarter, asked Alec, "Did you check that the plane to New York is going to be on time?"

Patrick answered for Alec with his German accent and said, "*Ja vol mein fraulein.* It's on time. Your flight is supposed to leave Portland at 12:20 PM and arrive in the Big Apple by 1:34 PM. What do you plan to do once you arrive? The flight to Copenhagen departs at 9:25 PM. That's an eight-hour layover!"

Alec agreed. "It's a long time to wait, but with our first-class tickets, we'll be able to relax at the airline's Sky Club until the flight. I understand members can use their free wi-fi, watch satellite TV, unwind in recliner chairs, and nosh on delicious food, beverages, and cocktails.

"We'll also be able to sleep on the plane. The first-class seats can turn into beds that recline 180 degrees. I plan on sleeping after the airline staff serves us our late dinner."

Irena giggled, "I'm going to feel like a queen. Thank you for upgrading our tickets from economy. It was generous of Gustav to pay for our flight and cruise, but I'm too old to sit upright in a plane for eight hours at nighttime."

"Speaking of Uncle Gustav," Paige remarked, "I just received an email from him. Do you want me to read it out loud from my phone?"

Alec said, "We're all ears. Go right ahead."

Paige squawked as she pressed the wrong icon in the moving car and replied, "Here it is and read aloud,

Subj: Upcoming Plans
Date: 4th of August, 08:58:07 PM UTC
From: GustavAnderson@aol.com
To: PaigeDunBarton@aol.com

Paige,

I was thrilled to hear that you're all coming on the family ancestor cruise. I spoke to your father the other day and he's anxious for us all to get together. Your dad, brother, and sister-in-law also plan to arrive in Copenhagen on Saturday, the 6th, sometime between two and three in the afternoon. I've taken the liberty to book three executive suites for the family at the Imperial Hotel on Vester Farimagsgade 9.

I assume you and your husband will be fine in one room, Derek and Gail will take the other, and Irena can share hers with Russell. Stefan is flying in from England and has insisted on having his own quarters. I'm sorry Aunt Jeanne won't be able to join us on this occasion. I plan to visit California in the near future and hope to see her then.

I believe you'll find the hotel suitable. It is centrally located and two-tenths of a mile from Tivoli Gardens. I made sure to include breakfast in your booking. I heard your husband is a good eater. As to my plans, I'm going to have a welcome party at one of the hotel's conference rooms on Sunday, the 7th of August.

You should be able to overcome any jetlag by then and still be able to enjoy a full day of sightseeing before we embark on our cruise Tuesday afternoon. The cruise itinerary is slightly different from the one I had originally sent you. I've inserted a copy.

Like most families, I'm afraid we see far too little of each other. You'll be happy to know that my two children will be joining us. Margaret, my eldest is a VP and major shareholder at Anderson's Biscuits. Justin is bringing along his mother (my former second wife).

As you may remember, Justin was raised in America and has a vegan food blog. He has shown no interest is helping his stepsister or me run the family business. The only other person coming on the cruise with us is my English social secretary, David Law. He's a genius at making arrangements and is quite indispensable to me.

I think I've told you everything you need to know. Kastrup Airport is only five and half miles from the hotel. As your plane is scheduled to arrive on Saturday at 11:30 AM our time, I've told the hotel when to expect you.

Please don't feel rushed. I expect Irena may want to nap. The old girl is getting on in age. If it's convenient for you, I would like us to get together for an informal dinner that night. I'll have David Law check in on you upon your arrival.

Have a safe trip,
Uncle Gustav

Paige was able to read the entire message despite hearing a few unladylike snorts from Irena. When Paige finished, her aunt complained, "I'll have you know, Gus is five years older than me. 'Old girl, my foot!'

"As to sharing a room with Russell, I think it will be fun. But Stefan has some nerve demanding his own quarters. It would have been far more normal for your father and Stefan to share and for me, the only woman, to have her own room."

Alec turned his body to gaze at Paige sitting in the backseat and asked, "Why is Justin bringing his mother? I can't imagine that Gustav wants his ex-wife hanging around. Is the boy very young?"

Paige laughed. "Justin is at least thirty. His mother, Regina Wolfe, used to be Gustav's personal secretary."

Irena interrupted, "She knows where all the bodies are buried."

Alec sat back in his seat and commented to Patrick, "I thought my family was full of strange characters. Now, I'm not so sure."

Eager to see how the itinerary changed, Alec asked Paige for her phone and opened the inserted file. Alec noticed a few slight differences as his eyes scanned the contents and read,

Centaurus Itinerary

Twelve-Day Baltic Tapestry Cruise
Copenhagen to Copenhagen

Date	Day	Port of Call	Arrival	Departure
9-Aug	Tue	Copenhagen, Denmark		4:00 PM
10-Aug	Wed	At Sea		
11-Aug	Thu	Oslo, Norway	7:00 AM	6:00 PM
12-Aug	Fri	Gothenburg, Sweden	7:00 AM	5:00 PM
13-Aug	Sat	Kiel (Hamburg), Germany	8:00 AM	6:00 PM
14-Aug	Sun	At Sea		
15-Aug	Mon	Visby, Gotland, Sweden	7:00 AM	6:00 PM
16-Aug	Tue	Stockholm, Sweden	7:00 AM	5:00 PM
17-Aug	Wed	St. Petersburg, Russia	7:00 AM	
18-Aug	Thu	St. Petersburg, Russia		6:00PM
19-Aug	Fri	At Sea		
20-Aug	Sat	Warnemunde, Germany	6:00 AM	8:00 PM
21-Aug	Sun	Copenhagen, Denmark	6:00 AM	

After confirming that they were still visiting the same ports and would be able go on the same excursions, their conversation turned to more mundane matters.

Although not mundane to Patrick, Alec recalled how brilliant Patrick had been while playing the part of Algernon Moncrieff in *The Importance of Being Ernest*. He, Paige, and Irena had spent a lovely evening watching him perform. The local newspaper reviewed it and wrote. "Watch out for Patrick Bishop. He's sure to be a rising star in the industry."

Still thinking about the night, Alec remarked, "I'm glad Hillary was able to return to Maine to see the performance and spend a few days with Walt."

Paige added, "Hillary told me that Leanne has been seeing a lot more of her sons in Portland and New York City. She and Hillary have gotten together for lunch a few times, and Leanne is thinking of getting a small apartment in Manhattan."

"I think the change will do her good," Irena acknowledged. "Leanne once told me that she wanted to do more with her life.

Being a doctor's wife shouldn't be a career in itself unless you want it to be."

Alec agreed and summed up, "Everything has worked out well. It looks like Alan Pierce will serve his sentence in Maine and be able to practice medicine in a reduced capacity at the prison. Hillary and Walt are enjoying their relationship, and Joan is excited about running the bed and breakfast."

After Patrick stopped the car in front of the airline's departure area at Portland International Jetport, he chimed in, "Don't forget me! I'm going to be a millionaire when probate is settled and will be starting college in a few weeks."

Irena kissed Patrick's cheek when everyone got out of the car and told him to behave while she was away. Once their luggage from the backseat and trunk were unloaded, Alec counted the number of pieces, the people in his traveling party, and the additional carry-on bags.

Assured that nothing was missing, Alec waved goodbye to Patrick and announced, "We're about to start another adventure! Let's get going."

Recipes from the B&B

▼

Almond Slices
Makes 24 to 28 Slices

Ingredients:

    2 eggs
    ⅔ cup granulated sugar
    ⅓ cup canola oil
    2 teaspoons almond extract
        2 cups all-purpose flour
        1½ teaspoons baking powder
            1½ cup fruits/nuts (can use an assortment of almonds, walnuts, pecans, raisins, currants, dates, apricots, cranberries, and chocolate chips)
            flour for shaping

Preheat the oven to 325°F. and line a cookie sheet with a piece of parchment paper. In a large bowl, beat the eggs well and add the sugar, oil, and almond extract.

Combine the flour and baking powder together and mix it into the egg mixture. Stir in a combination of chopped nuts, dried fruits, and chocolate chips. Let the dough stand 10 to 15 minutes to allow the dough to set.

Turn the mixture onto a floured board. Knead in just enough flour to make the dough pliable. Divide the dough in half. Shape each half into strips ½-inch thick, 3-inches wide and 12-inches long. Place them on the prepared cookie sheet.

Bake the strips for 30 to 35 minutes or until their edges begin to brown. Let cool 5 minutes. While they are warm, transfer them to a cutting board.

With a long-serrated knife, diagonally cut each strip into ½-inch slices. Unlike biscotti, these slices are richer, moister, and more crumbly. After the slices cool, store them in a metal tin. Almond Nut Slices also freeze well and can be served later.

****

Bacon and Cheddar Cheese Quiche
in a Hash Brown Potato Crust
Serves 6 to 8

Ingredients:

4 tablespoons butter
12 ounces shredded hash browns (fresh or defrosted and squeezed of excess liquid)
salt and pepper to taste
2 tablespoons butter
1½ cup onions, diced small
4 rashers or ½ cup crisply cooked bacon, crumbled
8 ounces or 2 cups sharp cheddar cheese, shredded
4 large eggs, beaten

1 cup heavy cream
½ cup half and half

Preheat the oven to 375°F. Thoroughly butter a deep-dish pie pan. In a medium-sized frying pan, melt the butter and sauté the shredded potatoes on high heat until they are golden brown and crispy. Salt and pepper to taste.

Remove from the frying pan and press the warm shredded potatoes onto the bottom and up the sides of the deep-dish pie pan. Cool while preparing the filling.

Add an additional 2 tablespoons of butter to the pan and sauté the onion until it becomes golden brown and has begun to caramelize. Set aside in a large mixing bowl.

In the same frying pan, brown the bacon until crispy. Let it cool and crumble the rashers into small pieces. It should measure about a half cup. Add it to the bowl containing the onions.

To the onion and bacon bowl, add the beaten eggs, heavy cream, half and half, and cheddar cheese. Mix well, Add salt and pepper to taste.

Spoon the cheese mixture over the chilled potato crust. Bake the quiche for 40 to 45 minutes or until the rim is brown and the top is firm. Let it cool for 5 minutes before cutting.

The Bacon and Cheddar Cheese Quiche can be served a day later and warmed in the microwave. It can also be frozen, thawed, and microwaved at another time.

****

Baked Apple French Toast
Serves 4 to 6

Ingredients:

2 to 3 Granny Smith apples (reduce sugar if not using tart apples
½ stick butter
⅓ cup firmly packed dark brown sugar
2 teaspoons cinnamon
1 loaf French bread or challah
6 eggs
1½ cups whole milk or half and half
1 tablespoon vanilla extract

Preheat the oven to 350°F. Grease a 9x13-inch glass baking dish and place a piece of parchment paper on the bottom. Quarter and core the apples. There is no need to peel them. Cut each quarter into 6 to 8 slices (⅛ thin).

In a small saucepan, melt the butter and add the brown sugar and cinnamon. Mix well. Cook over medium heat until the mixture becomes syrupy.

Pour the syrup onto the prepared 9x13-inch glass baking dish. Arrange the apple slices over the syrup mixture in an attractive design.

Slice the French bread or challah into 1-inch-thick pieces. Place the bread over the apple slices. In a medium-sized bowl, beat the eggs, and add the milk and vanilla extract. Mix well and pour the egg mixture evenly over the bread.

Bake uncovered for 40 to 45 minutes. After the Baked Apple French Toast cools slightly, carefully invert the baking dish over a large platter and remove the parchment paper to reveal the apple slices. Leftovers can be microwaved the following day.

****

Banana Walnut Bread
Makes 12 muffins or 1 (9x5x3-inch) loaf

Ingredients:

1⅓ cup overripe bananas (3 large), mashed
⅓ cup salted butter, melted
1¾ cups all-purpose flour
¾ cup granulated sugar
1 teaspoon baking soda
1 large egg, beaten
2 teaspoons vanilla extract
1 cup walnuts, coarsely chopped

Preheat the oven to 350°F. Grease the muffin tins and line each cup with a small circular piece of parchment paper. Do not use cupcake liners as they will stick to the banana bread.

In a large bowl, mash the bananas with a fork or a potato masher until they're almost completely smooth. Retain 1⅓ cups of the mashed bananas and add the melted butter.

Combine the flour, sugar, and baking soda together. Stir the dry ingredients into the banana mixture. Stir in the egg and vanilla and mix well. Fold in the coarsely chopped walnuts. The batter will be thick.

Bake the muffins for 25 to 30 minutes or until a cake tester comes out clean and the banana bread is golden brown. Let the muffins cool in the pan before placing them on a cooling rack. Remove the parchment paper before serving.

The banana bread can also be baked in a 9x5x3-inch loaf pan at 325°F. for 45-50 minutes. Both the muffins and loaf freeze well and can be warmed and served at a later time.

****

Cheese Danish
Makes 18 small Danishes

Ingredients:

> 1 17.3-ounce box frozen puff pastry
> 8 ounces cream cheese, softened
> ⅓ cup granulated sugar
> 1 egg yolk
> 1 tablespoon fresh lemon juice
> 1 teaspoon vanilla extract
>> fruit jam, if desired
>> egg wash (beaten egg with 1 tablespoon of water)
>> powdered sugar, if desired

Defrost the box of frozen puff pastry sheets and thaw for 50 minutes. Keep it in the refrigerator until needed. Preheat the oven to 400°F. Line the cookie sheet with parchment paper.

In a medium-sized bowl, cream the softened cream cheese with the sugar until the mixture is smooth. Add the egg yolk, lemon juice, and vanilla extract. Mix well.

Remove one pastry sheet from the refrigerator. Unfold the 9x9-inch sheet and place it on a floured board. With a butter knife, divide the 9x9-inch pastry into 3x3-inch squares so there are a total of 9 squares. With a floured rolling pin, flatten the dough slightly and make sure the squares are even on all sides.

Spoon a heaping tablespoon of the cream cheese mixture in the center of the square. If desired, a half teaspoon of fruit jam can be spooned on top of the cheese mixture.

The Danishes can be shaped in three ways: bring up each corner of the square, leaving exposed cream cheese and jam in the center; shape the square into a triangle and crimped along the two open edges; or, fold the opposite sides of the square over the cheese mixture, leaving two exposed areas.

Repeat with the second puffed pastry sheet. Place the Danishes on the lined baking sheet and brush the pastry tops with an egg wash (1 beaten egg with 1 tablespoon of water).

Bake the pastries for 15 to 18 minutes or until they are puffed, sizzling, and golden brown. If desired, the Danishes can be dusted with powdered sugar while warm. The pastries are best when freshly baked but can be frozen without the confection's sugar and served later.

****

Chocolate Chip Dream Bars
(*Gluten Free*)
Makes 21 to 24 bars (3x1 inches)

Ingredients:
- 1¾ cups almond or rice flour
- ⅓ cup firmly packed brown sugar
- 1 stick salted butter
- 3 large eggs
- ½ cup firmly packed dark brown sugar
- ⅓ cup honey
- ⅓ cup almond or rice flour
- ¾ teaspoon baking powder
- 1½ teaspoons vanilla extract
- ¾ cup semisweet chocolate morsels
- ¾ cup moist shredded coconut

Preheat the oven to 350°F. Grease an 8x8- or 9x9-inch square cake pan and line the bottom with a piece of parchment paper. In a medium-sized bowl, combine the gluten-free flour with the brown sugar.

Work in the cold butter with a pastry blender or two butter knives until the mixture is crumbly. Gather it together with your hands and pat it firmly into the prepared cake pan. Bake the layer for 15 to 20 minutes or until the base has begun to brown.

While the bottom layer is baking, prepare the topping. In a medium-sized bowl, beat the eggs until frothy and mix in the brown sugar. Stir in the honey, gluten-free flour, baking powder, and vanilla extract. Mix only till blended.

Fold in the chocolate chips and flaked coconut. Pour the mixture evenly over the partially baked bottom layer.

Return the cake pan to the oven to bake an additional 30 minutes or until the Chocolate Chip Dream Bars are puffy and golden brown.

Cool thoroughly and cut into slices (3-inches long by 1-inch wide). Chocolate Chip Dream Bars can be stored for a week in a metal tin or frozen to be served later.

****

Cinnamon Crescent Rolls
Makes 8 crescent rolls

Ingredients:
ʼ¼ cup firmly packed dark brown sugar
2 teaspoons cinnamon
¾ cup pecan pieces, chopped fine
1 8-ounce tube crescent roll dough
3 tablespoons butter, melted

Preheat the oven to 375°F. Line a cookie sheet with parchment paper. In a small bowl, combine the brown sugar, cinnamon, and chopped pecans.

Separate the crescent dough sheet into eight elongated triangles and brush with melted butter Sprinkle the nut mixture evenly over them. Roll up, going from the wider end to the narrow point.

Brush the tops of each crescent roll with the melted butter and dip it into the remaining nut mixture. Bend the ends of the rolls to form a crescent shape.

Bake for 10 to 12 minutes or until the rolls are crisp and golden brown. Serve warm. Leftovers can be warmed in the microwave.

****

Cranberry Pumpkin Bread
Serves 16 (one-inch slices)

Ingredients:
>2 cups all-purpose flour
>⅔ cup granulated sugar
>1 tablespoon pumpkin pie spice
>2 teaspoons baking soda
>¼ teaspoon salt
>>1 cup pure pumpkin
>>3 eggs, beaten
>>⅔ cup canola oil
>>¼ cup orange juice
>>>½ cup dried cranberries (cut in half)

Preheat the oven to 325°F. Grease and flour a 10-inch Bundt pan. In a large-sized bowl, combine the flour, sugar, pumpkin pie spice, baking soda, and salt.

Add the pumpkin, beaten eggs, oil, and orange juice, and mix until blended. Fold in the dried cranberries that have been cut in half.

Spoon the batter into a prepared 10-inch Bundt pan. Bake for 40 to 50 minutes or until the cake tester, inserted in the cracks, comes out clean. Lightly cover the cake with a piece of aluminum foil if the top of the bread browns too quickly.

Let the bread cool completely before inverting the Bundt pan and removing the bread. The cranberry pumpkin batter can also be baked in muffin tins for 25 to 30 minutes at 350°F. Both the loaf and muffins freeze well and can be served at a later time.

****

Fruit Blintz Soufflé
Serves 4

Ingredients:
 1 package of frozen Golden Cherry or Blueberry Blintzes (6 blintzes)
 1 tablespoon salted butter
  3 eggs, beaten
  1 cup sour cream
  ½ cup heavy cream
  4 tablespoons firmly packed dark brown sugar
  1 teaspoon vanilla extract
  ½ teaspoon cinnamon
  ⅛ teaspoon cardamom
   sour cream, if desired

Defrost the frozen cherry or blueberry blintzes for 30 minutes. Cut the blintzes into bite-sized slices. Preheat the oven to 350°F. Melt a tablespoon of butter in a 2-quart soufflé or casserole dish. Place the blintze slices, cut side up, in two layers on the bottom of the dish.

In a medium-sized bowl, mix together the beaten eggs, sour cream, heavy cream, brown sugar, vanilla extract, cinnamon and cardamom. Pour the mixture over the blintzes.

Bake for about 1¼ hours (check after an hour). When done, the soufflé will be puffy and golden brown.

Serve while hot with cold sour cream. The Fruit Blintz Soufflé will collapse upon cooling. The egg mixture can be prepared the night before and baked with the blintzes the following morning to save time.

****

Grandma's Date-Nut Bread
Makes 8 mini-loaves or 1 large loaf (8 to 12 slices)

Ingredients:
>   1 stick salted butter
>   1 cup water
>   ¾ cup granulated sugar
>   1 cup pitted dates or prunes, diced into ¼-inch pieces
>   2 large eggs
>   2 cups all-purpose flour
>   1 teaspoon baking soda
>   1 teaspoon baking powder
>   1 cup walnuts, coarsely chopped
>   1 tablespoon brandy

Preheat the oven to 325°F and grease a loaf pan that contains 8 individual loaves. Line each with a small rectangular piece of parchment paper.

In a medium-sized saucepan, place the butter, water, sugar, and dates. Heat gently until the butter melts and the sugar dissolves. Remove it from the heat and let the mixture cool for 10 minutes.

Beat the eggs in a large bowl until frothy. Add the date mixture. Stir well. Combine the flour and baking soda. Add the dry ingredients to the date and egg mixture. Mix until blended. The batter will be slightly lumpy. Fold in the walnuts and the brandy.

Scoop the batter into the mini loaves, up to two-thirds full. Bake for 30-35 minutes or until a cake tester inserted in the centers come out clean.

The Date Nut Bread can also be baked in a lined 9x5x3-inch loaf pan at 325°F and will take 55 to 65 minutes. The bread will keep for several days and freezes well.

****

Ham and Cheese Parcels
Serves 6 to 8

Ingredients:

2 8-ounce packages of crescent sheet dough (not precut)
2 tablespoons butter
1 cup Vidalia onions, diced small
1 cup button mushrooms, diced small
6 ounces maple honey ham or low-salt ham, finely chopped
1 cup Swiss cheese, shredded
1 cup Gruyere or Fontina cheese, shredded
⅓ cup pitted black olives, sliced

Unroll the first crescent dough sheet and place it on a piece of parchment paper. Smooth the dough out so it measures 9x12-inches. Preheat the oven to 375°F.

Melt the butter in medium-sized frying pan and sauté the diced onions and mushrooms until they are golden brown and have begun to caramelize (about 10 minutes). Set aside.

In a medium-sized bowl, combine the ham, cheeses, olives, sautéed onions, and mushrooms. Divide the mixture into two equal portions.

Mound one portion of the cheese mixture in the middle third of the first crescent dough sheet, leaving 1 inch to 1½ inches of unfilled pastry on the top and bottom. Fold the top and bottom pastry over the cheese mixture.

Cut the sides of the unfolded pastry into 6 horizontal strips on both sides of the cheese mixture. To complete, place the right cut strip over the filling at a diagonal, alternating each side to make an attractive pattern.

When folded the Ham and Cheese Parcel will be about 4 to 5 inches wide and 7 to 8 inches long. Make 4 slits in the center of the pastry to allow the steam to escape. Transfer the parcel and parchment paper to a baking sheet. Brush with an egg wash (1 beaten egg with 1 tablespoon water).

Repeat with the second crescent dough sheet. Mound the remaining filling in the middle third of the sheet and make another parcel. Place it beside the first parcel.

Bake the pastries for 18-22 minutes or until the crust is golden brown. The cheese filling can be prepared the day before, chilled overnight, and baked the following morning to save time.

****

Honey Spice Cake
Serves 16 (one-inch slices)

Ingredients:

<u>Ingredients:</u>

    1 stick salted butter
    1 tablespoon water
    ¾ cup honey
    ½ cup firmly packed dark brown sugar
        2 cups all-purpose flour
        1 teaspoon baking powder
        ½ teaspoon baking soda
        1 teaspoon cinnamon
        ½ teaspoon ginger
        ¼ teaspoon cloves
        ⅛ teaspoon cardamom
            ½ cup sour cream
            3 large eggs, beaten
                powdered sugar, if desired

Preheat the oven to 350°F. Grease a 10-inch tube pan and line the bottom with a circular piece of parchment paper that has a 2-inch hole in the center.

In a small saucepan, place the butter, water, honey, and brown sugar. Heat gently until the butter melts and the sugar dissolves. Remove it from the heat and let the mixture cool for 10 minutes.

In a large bowl, combine the flour, baking powder, and baking soda. Add the four spices. Make a well in the center of the dry ingredients and pour the honey mixture into the center. Be sure to scrape up any honey that may have settled at the bottom of the saucepan. Add the sour cream and mix until smooth. Fold in the beaten eggs.

Pour the batter into the prepared tube pan and bake for 40-50 minutes or until a cake tester inserted in the center comes out clean. Let cool. Serve as is or dust with powdered sugar. The Honey Spice Cake will keep for several days and freezes well.

****

Irena's Waffles with Fruit Compotes
Serves 4 (2 waffles each)

Ingredients for the Waffles:
>   2 cups all-purpose flour
>   2 tablespoons granulated sugar
>   1 tablespoon baking powder
>   ⅓ cup melted salted butter or vegetable oil
>   1¾ cups whole or 2% milk
>   2 large eggs
>   ½ teaspoon vanilla extract

For the Waffles: In a large bowl, combine the flour, sugar, and baking powder. Add the milk, eggs, and vanilla. Mix well and add the butter or oil. Blend until smooth.

Follow the directions on the waffle maker. For best results, serve immediately. The waffles can also be warmed in a 200°F. oven until ready to serve.

Ingredients for the Fruit Compote:
>   2 to 3 cups of fresh diced fruit (leave blueberries whole)
>   ¼ cup water (or juice from the fruit)
>   1 tablespoon granulated sugar
>   ¼ teaspoon almond extract
>   2 teaspoons cornstarch dissolved in 2 tablespoons water
>   1 teaspoon fresh lemon juice

For the Fruit Compote (Blueberry, Strawberry, Cherry, and, and Peach): Combine the diced fresh fruit in a medium saucepan with water (or juice from the fruit), sugar, and almond extract.

Cook on a low heat until the fruit softens and loses some of its shape. Add the cornstarch, which was dissolved in 2 tablespoons of water. Heat until the mixture thickens. Add the lemon juice.

Serve the compote warm and pour on top of the waffles or in an accompanying bowl beside the waffles. The compote can be made a few days ahead and refrigerated until ready to heat and serve.

****

Karine's Cinnamon Babka
Serves 16 (one-inch slices)

Ingredients for the Dough:
> ½ cup whole milk
> ¼ cup water
> 1 teaspoon granulated sugar
> 2 packets dry yeast (¼ ounce each)
> 1 stick salted butter
> ¾ cup granulated sugar
> 4 egg yolks (reserve 1 egg white for wash)
> 1½ teaspoons vanilla extract
> 2¾ to 3¼ cups all-purpose flour

Ingredients for the Filling:
> 2½ cups ground walnuts
> 1 cup firmly packed dark brown sugar
> 1½ tablespoons cinnamon
> ¼ teaspoon cardamom
> 6 tablespoons salted butter

In a small saucepan, warm the water and milk. Add the sugar and let it dissolve. The mixture should be warmer than lukewarm and a bit hot to the touch (110°F.).

Pour the mixture into a large glass bowl. Dissolve 2 packets of dry yeast (¼ ounce each) into the milk mixture. Over the next few minutes, the yeast mixture should become foamy. If it doesn't, the milk was either too hot or the yeast too old. You will need to dispose of it and start again with new ingredients,

In the same saucepan, melt the butter. Add the sugar and stir until the sugar dissolves. Add the egg yolks, one at a time and beat in. Mix in the vanilla extract. While still warm but not hot, add it to the yeast mixture.

Measure out 2¾ cups of flour and stir into the butter/yeast mixture until combined. Add an additional tablespoon of flour, one at a time, and mix until a soft dough forms. It should be tacky but not wet or sticky.

Once a soft dough forms, transfer it to a floured surface, and knead it until it becomes a smooth ball. Do not over knead. Place the dough into a buttered mixing bowl and cover with plastic wrap. Refrigerate overnight.

On the day of baking, remove the dough from the refrigerator and allow it to warm for 30 minutes. While it's sitting, combine the ground nuts, sugar, and cinnamon.

Melt the butter in a small saucepan and let it cool. Once the dough has warmed slightly, divide it in half and roll the first half out on a floured surface to form a 12x18-inch rectangle.

Brush half the melted butter onto the rolled dough and sprinkle a little less than half the sugar/nut mixture evenly over it. Roll the 18-inch side tightly and twist the log.

Repeat with the second half of the dough. When you have two 18-inch twisted rolls, gently twist them together to form one large-twisted roll.

Place the dough in a 10-inch buttered tube pan that has been lined with a circular piece of parchment paper. Cover the pan with a tea towel and allow it to rise for an hour or two in a warm place.

Preheat the oven to 350°F. When Karine's Cinnamon Babka completely fills the pan, poke a few holes in the dough with a thin skewer to allow steam to escape and to prevent large air holes from forming inside the cake.

Brush the top of the babka with an egg wash (1 egg white and 1 tablespoon of water). Sprinkle the remaining cinnamon and nut mixture over it.

Bake for 45 to 50 minutes or until the babka is golden brown and sounds hollow when tapped. Do not slice the babka until completely cool as the filling needs to set. Babka can be stored in a metal tin for a few days and can be frozen to be served later.

****

Patrick's Irish Soda Bread
Serves 6 to 8

Ingredients:
<u>Ingredients:</u>
     2 cups all-purpose flour
     3 tablespoons sugar
     ½ teaspoon baking soda
     ½ teaspoon cream of tartar
     1 stick salted butter
     ½ cup raisins
     1 tablespoon caraway seeds
     ⅔ cup buttermilk or ⅔ cup milk and 2 teaspoons vinegar
     1 large egg, lightly beaten

Preheat the oven to 375°F. Grease a 9-inch pie pan and line with a circular piece of parchment paper. In a large bowl, combine the flour, sugar, baking soda, and cream of tartar. Mix well.

Cut in the butter until the mixture resembles coarse corn meal. Add the buttermilk and beaten egg all at once. Stir with a fork until just blended. Knead lightly, about 10 times with additional flour so it forms a ball.

Turn onto a buttered 9-inch pie plate, mounding the mixture in the center. With a knife, cut an X on the top, about a ½-inch deep, so you can see four evenly sized quarters.

Bake for 30 to 40 minutes or until a cake tester comes out clean. When thumped, the bread should sound hollow. Cut into wedges when slightly warm and serve with butter and jam. Patrick's Irish Soda Bread is best when freshly baked. Leftovers can be frozen and warmed later in the oven or microwave.

****

Peach and Apple Turnovers
Makes 18 small pastries per box

Ingredients for the Peach Turnovers:
> 1 17.3-ounce frozen package of puff pastry sheets
> flour for rolling
> 3 cups unpeeled peached, diced small
> 2 tablespoons brown sugar
> 1 tablespoon cornstarch
> 1 teaspoon cinnamon
> egg wash (1 beaten egg with 1 tablespoon water)
> powdered sugar

Ingredients for the Apple Filling:
> 2 cups unpeeled apples, diced small
> ⅓ cup water
> 2 tablespoons firmly packed brown sugar
> 1 teaspoon cinnamon

Defrost the box of frozen pastry sheets and thaw for about 50 minutes in the refrigerator. Preheat the oven to 400°F. and line a baking sheet with a piece of parchment paper.

Cut the unpeeled peaches into ½-inch slices and dice each slice into 4 smaller pieces. In a medium-sized bowl, place the peaches, sugar, cornstarch, and cinnamon. Mix until the peaches are coated and set aside.

For the apples, combine the ingredients in a small saucepan and cook on low heat until the apples soften, and the mixture thickens. Set aside.

Remove one pastry sheet from the refrigerator. Unfold the 9x9-inch sheet and place it on a floured board. With a butter knife, divide the 9x9-inch pastry into 3x3-inch squares so there are a total of 9 squares. With a floured rolling pin, make sure the squares are even on all sides.

Spoon about a tablespoon of the peach or apple filling in the center of a square and fold over one corner to form a triangle. Press the open sides down with your fingers and crimp the edges with the tines of a fork that were dipped in flour. Do the same with the remaining 8 squares.

Repeat the process with the second pastry sheet. Place the turnovers on a cookie sheet that has been lined with parchment paper. Brush the tops of each turnover with the egg wash. Prick the tops with a fork to allow the steam to escape. Bake for 15 minutes or until they are puffed, sizzling, and golden brown.

Dust the turnovers with powdered sugar while still warm. The turnovers are best when freshly baked. They can be frozen without confectioners' sugar and dusted before serving. Both the peach and apple filling can be prepared and refrigerated a day or two before baking.

****

Pecan Pie Squares
Serves 12 to 16

Ingredients:
>   2¾ cup all-purpose flour
>   ½ cup granulated sugar
>   1½ sticks salted butter
>   5 eggs beaten (1¼ cups)
>   1 cup light corn syrup
>   ¾ cup firmly packed brown sugar
>   6 tablespoons melted salted butter
>   3 tablespoons all-purpose flour
>   2 tablespoons brandy or whisky
>   1½ teaspoons vanilla extract
>   1 teaspoon almond extract
>   1 teaspoon cinnamon
>   2½ cups pecan halves or pieces

Preheat the oven to 350°F. Butter a 9x13-inch glass baking dish. In a large-sized bowl, mix together the flour and sugar. Cut in the butter until it resembles cornmeal.

Form the mixture into a soft dough ball and pat onto the bottom of the baking dish. Bake for 20 minutes or until the crust is a light golden brown. Let cool while preparing the filling.

To make the filling, beat the eggs in a large-sized bowl. Add the corn syrup, brown sugar, melted butter, flour, brandy, vanilla extract, almond extract, and cinnamon. Mix well. Fold in the pecans.

Spread the pecan mixture evenly over the parbaked crust. Bake an additional 25 to 30 minutes or until the Pecan Pie Squares are puffy and the top is set.

Cool on a wire rack. Cut into squares and serve with a dollop of whipped cream. The Pecan Pie Squares can be frozen and served at a later time.

Rich Tea Scones
Makes 6 large or 9 medium scones

Ingredients:

    2 cups all-purpose flour
    ⅓ cup granulated sugar
    1½ teaspoons baking powder
    1 teaspoon baking soda
        6 tablespoons cold salted butter
        1 large egg, beaten
        ½ cup sour cream
            flour for rolling
            egg wash (1 beaten egg with 1 tablespoon water)
            strawberry, raspberry, or apricot jam
            whipped cream

Preheat the oven to 375°F. Place a piece of parchment paper onto a cookie sheet. In a large bowl, combine the flour, sugar, baking powder, and baking soda.

Cut in the cold butter with a pastry blender or two butter knives until the mixture is crumbly and resembles the texture of cornmeal. Add the beaten egg and sour cream to the flour mixture.

Stir with a fork until large chunks begin to form and adhere to one another. Gently knead the dough together with your hands just until it forms a soft ball.

Roll or pat the dough on a floured surface until it measures 1-inch high. With a floured glass or biscuit cutter, cut out the scones (do not twist the glass or cutter as it will prevent the scone from rising properly).

Place them on the prepared cookie sheet. A 2½-inch cutter will yield about 6 scones and a 2-inch cutter, approximately 9 scones. Brush the top of the scones with an egg wash.

Bake for 15 to 18 minutes or until the bottom of the scones are golden brown. Serve them fresh from the oven with jam and whipped cream. They can also be frozen and warmed later in the oven or microwave.

****

Sausage, Spinach, Cheese Frittata
Serves 4

Ingredients:
      6 large eggs, beaten
      ¼ cup heavy cream
      salt and pepper to taste
          2 tablespoons butter
          1 tablespoon oil
          1 cup shredded hash brown potatoes
          1 large onion, diced
               4 fully cooked pork or turkey sausage links, sliced
               2 cups fresh leaf spinach
               1 cup shredded sharp cheddar or Swiss cheese
                    ¼ cup scallions, diced
                    paprika

Preheat the oven to 400°F. In a small bowl, whisk the eggs with heavy cream. Add salt and pepper to taste and set aside the bowl.

To a heated 10-inch cast iron skillet pan, add the butter and oil. After the butter melts, sauté the onions and potatoes until they turn golden brown.

Add the sliced sausages, followed by the spinach. Stir the mixture until the spinach greens wilt. Flatten the sausages and vegetables in the skillet with a spatula and evenly sprinkle the cheddar cheese over the mixture.

When the cheese begins to melt, slowly pour the beaten egg mixture over the sausage and vegetables and tilt the pan to fill up any empty spaces. Cook for a minute or two or until you see the eggs at the edge of the pan start to set.

Transfer the skillet to the preheated oven. Bake the frittata for 8 to 10 minutes. To check whether fully cooked, cut a small slit into the center of the frittata. If raw egg fills the slit, bake for a few more minutes.

Let the frittata cool on the stove top for five minutes. Garnish with scallions and paprika. Cut into 4 wedges and serve hot.

For a Sausage, Broccoli, and Cheese Frittata: Replace the spinach with sautéed chopped broccoli. Can also exchange the onions with diced, fresh peppers. Otherwise cook as directed.

****

Sour Cream Coffee Cake
Serves 16 (one-inch slices)

Ingredients:
>2 sticks salted butter
>1¼ cups granulated sugar
>3 large eggs
>2 teaspoons vanilla extract
>>2 cups all-purpose flour
>>1½ teaspoons baking powder
>>1 teaspoon baking soda

1 cup sour cream
½ cup chopped walnuts
⅓ cup firmly packed dark brown sugar
1 tablespoon cinnamon

Preheat the oven to 350°F. Grease a 10-inch tube pan and line the bottom with a circular piece of parchment paper.

In a large bowl, cream the butter until it is light and fluffy. Add the sugar and mix until it's of spreading consistency. Beat the eggs until they are frothy and add the vanilla extract. Slowly pour the eggs into the creamed mixture and stir well.

Combine the flour, baking powder, and baking soda. Mix one third of the dry ingredients into the butter mixture alternately with the sour cream, (beginning and ending with dry ingredients). Mix until blended. The batter will be thick.

Spoon the batter into the tube pan. Combine the chopped walnuts, sugar, and cinnamon together in a small bowl. Drizzle two thirds of it onto the batter. With a butter knife, swirl the sugar topping into the batter so that most of it has disappeared from the surface. Top with the remaining one-third mixture.

Bake for 40-50 minutes, or until the cake has started to pull away from the sides of the tube pan and an inserted cake tester comes out clean. Let it cool thoroughly before removing from the pan. The Sour Cream Coffee Cake will keep for several days and freezes well.

****

Swiss Cheese, Spinach Quiche
Serves 6 to 8

Ingredients:
1 deep dish pie crust, store bought or homemade
1 tablespoon butter

4 ounces or 1 cup button mushrooms, sliced
5 ounces fresh baby spinach
4 large eggs
1 cup heavy cream
½ cup half and half
salt and pepper to taste
8 ounces or 2 cups Swiss cheese, shredded

Preheat the oven to 425°F. Prepare the crust as instructed and place it in a 9-inch-deep dish pie pan. Crimp the edges. Prick the bottom and sides of the pan with a fork to allow the steam to escape.

Bake the crust in the oven for 15 minutes or until the pastry is golden brown. Let the pie shell cool and lower the oven temperature to 375°F.

While the pie crust is cooling, sauté the mushrooms in a tablespoon of butter until golden, about 8 to 10 minutes. Add the fresh baby spinach until it wilts. Place the mushroom and spinach mixture into of the pre-baked pie crust.

In a large bowl, whisk together the eggs, heavy cream, and half and half. Salt and pepper to taste. Add the shredded cheese and stir well. Pour the egg mixture on top of the mushrooms and spinach.

Bake at 375°F. for 50 to 55 minutes or until the quiche is firm to the touch and golden brown. Serve warm.

Copyright Acknowledgments

▼

SUMMER BREEZE

THE END OF INNOCENCE

THERE IS A MOUNTAIN